"What an awful place this is," Babs said.

"Nonsense. This is swinging London," I told her. I was trying to mask my intentions, but I knew that she was going to ask the inevitable.

"Why are we here?"

"To see how the other half lives."

"C'mon, honey, I want to know."

"There is a man here I want to see."

"What sort of man?"

"A man who wears fancy hats and sells heroin to kids."

She nodded and leaned back in her chair, a troubled expression on her face. It was obvious that she knew what I was planning. I could see that she wanted to say Don't do it, let's go home, forget it. But what she didn't know is that I had to do it, I couldn't go home—because it was something I'd never forget. . . .

The Big Needle

KEN FOLLETT

WRITING AS SYMON MYLES

ZEBRA BOOKS
KENSINGTON PUBLISHING CORP.

To Mary,
for six good years

ZEBRA BOOKS

are published by

KENSINGTON PUBLISHING CORP.
475 Park Avenue South
New York, N.Y. 10016

Copyright © 1975 by Ken Follett

Originally published in Great Britain by Everest Books
Ltd., 1974

Thirteenth printing: April, 1989

Printed in the United States of America

CHAPTER ONE

The air in the bedroom was cold when I poked my nose over the edge of the quilt. I wondered whether the central heating had gone on the blink. Either that or I had awakened at some uncivilised hour. I gently extricated my hand from underneath Babs. Her weight had cut off the circulation, and my arm felt like a lump of nerveless rubber. I waited for the blood to flow and the feeling to return. Then I looked at my watch. It was 5:30 a.m.

I said: "Bollocks."

Babs' head of dark Afro curls shuddered like a shaken hedge. She mumbled: "What are you cursing about," and went back to sleep before I could answer.

I wondered what had awakened me. On the other side of me from Babs there was a lump in the bed which was Annabel. I pulled the quilt back from her face. Underneath her slightly Roman nose, her wide mouth was open, showing her perfect teeth. She was snoring like a pig's grandmother—only a true aristocrat like Lady Annabel Dath could have outrageous manners and get away with it so graciously—but I had slept through the noise many times.

It wasn't like me to wake up early. It was still pretty dark outside, and there was not much noise up here on the fortieth floor. Normally I had trouble waking at 8:30. I wondered what had happened. Then it happened again. The doorbell rang.

I had wired it to play a few bars of blues, which was a great conversation piece but no consolation at the crack of dawn. I reached over Babs and picked up the telephone. I pressed a button marked "Front door". It connected me with a speaker beside the doorbell.

"There is nobody in," I said. "Go away. This is a recording."

A woman's voice said: "Open the door, Apples." Apples is my name, for reasons I'll get around to sometime. I slid down the bed between the sheets and rolled off the end of the divan.

I fumbled around in the semi-darkness for a robe. On the floor I found one dress, one blouse, two pairs of knickers—but no robe. Hell, I thought, whoever calls at this time of the day can't complain. I went naked.

There was a short passage between the bedroom and the living room. Off on the right were three rooms. They had been designed as a dining room, a second bedroom and a nursery; but we had made them into three studies—one each—for when we wanted to be alone.

I went into the living room and turned on the light. I screwed up my eyes against the glare—every damn thing in there was white: walls, carpet, curtains, furniture. On the far side of the room were two doors. One led to the kitchen. I went in there and switched on the central heating, the coffee pot and the toaster. I wondered who it was at the door. The voice had been familiar, but I couldn't quite place it.

6

I went out of the kitchen into the living room and through the other door to the hall. I opened the front door.

There stood Marjory. My ex-wife. Plus boy friend.

The boy friend was lean, suntanned, and about twenty years my junior. Suddenly I remembered my pot belly and scraggy legs.

Marjory said: "Hello, Apples."

"You'd better come in," I muttered ungraciously. Something was wrong. Catching me like that, Marjory ought to have said something sarcastic—but there had not even been a gleam of triumph in her eye.

They followed me into the living room. Babs was standing there, rubbing the sleep from her eyes. "Apples, what are you doing?" she yawned. Then, when she saw the other two: "Oh, excuse me."

The boy friend's eyes nearly popped out at the sight of her bare backside scampering through the door. My dignity was somewhat restored. "Sit down a minute," I told them, and went to get my trousers.

With my embarrassment covered I went back to face Marjory. I sat opposite the two of them in a trendy, plastic and horribly uncomfortable chair Annabel had designed. It had won some art award or other, but the judging panel didn't have to sit on it. I found a bent Gauloise in my pocket, stuck it in my mouth, and lit a match.

Marjory said: "Apples, Jane is in hospital in a coma."

I dropped the flaring match. Paralysed, I watched it burn a big brown hole in the carpet. Then I gently trod on it with my bare heel. I felt no pain. Jane was my seventeen-year-old daughter.

"How?"

"She injected herself with an overdose of heroin."

"Oh, Jesus, no." I struck another match, got the cigarette alight, and took a lungful. Straight away I felt nauseous. I fought it down.

"How is she going to be?"

Marjory looked at me, and now there was a bitter accusation in her eyes. "She may die."

Without apologising I got up and left the room. I went to the bathroom, wanting to throw up, but there was nothing in me. I felt sick, weak, and terribly guilty. I sat on the seat of the w.c. for a while, then I drank a glass of water and went back.

I said: "Why, Marjory? Have you any idea?"

"No. I've only seen her once in about a year. She wrote occasionally, always from a different address. Since she got thrown out of school—"

"Thrown out? You never told me!" I said bitterly.

"You never asked," she said quietly. It was true.

"Anyway, she said she was getting a little acting work, living in bedsitters; and finding out what life was all about." Marjory began to cry. "Apples, what could I do? She was a very mature seventeen, and they're adults at eighteen now. Should I have dragged her home by the hair?"

"No," I said, "no." I picked up another cigarette, then changed my mind.

There was a low whistle from the kitchen. The boy friend looked up, startled. "That's the coffee-maker," I told him. "Er . . . would you like some?"

Marjory shook her head. Her composure was returning, and she did not like being in my den of iniquity. Her father would have referred to my flat as the fleshpots of Babylon, and Marjory would have agreed, although she might not have used those words. "We'll go, Apples," she said.

She took a pen and an envelope from her handbag and scribbled the name of a hospital and a ward number. "Perhaps you'll go and see her," she said, handing me the scrap of paper. The sarcasm in her voice hardly registered with me, I was so stunned. The two of them stood up.

"Ah, just a minute," I stammered. "Um, is she having the best, you know . . ." I looked at the piece of paper. "Is she in a private ward, and everything?"

"Yes."

"Get the bill sent to me. No, I'll tell them when I go."

"It's all right. I already told them." The old bitterness came out in that sentence. In the ten years we had been divorced, we had met very few times: but whenever we did, we quarrelled about alimony.

I showed them to the door. "Thanks, for coming around here," I said. I shut the door.

I poured myself some coffee and sat on a stool in the kitchen, sipping the hot black liquid and shivering. I tried to picture Jane. Now she would be lying on a white hospital bed, her eyes closed, breathing shallowly. But did she have long hair or short? Was she suntanned? How tall was she? The last time I had seen her, she won the 100 metres sprint in the second form sports. She had long skinny legs and the beginnings of a woman's figure then. After I left Marjory I had only seen Jane on occasions like that. The girl had seemed to sympathise with her mother. Of course Marjory didn't tell her the full story—but

I didn't either: you couldn't explain that sort of thing to a child. Maybe I should have tried.

Marjory and I broke up because she wanted to grow old gracefully, and I just didn't want to grow old. As Jane began to grow up, she seemed ill at ease with me, and I hadn't pressed my company on her. She had become quite a sportswoman for a while—something she certainly did not inherit from her father, whose only sport was poker—she did well at school, and she was healthy.

But normal, healthy girls do not become heroin addicts. No doubt they all experiment with soft drugs: but just as most people drink all their lives without becoming alcoholics, so with drugs. There has to be something wrong before you move on to the hard stuff. What was wrong with Jane?

I poured more coffee. I was kidding myself. Jane came from a broken home. Growing up in an atmosphere of love is something most kids take for granted, and I had deprived her of that.

In the business world I was known as an achiever—a winner. But I had fouled up my most important project.

I went into the bedroom to get my clothes. Babs and Annabel were in a sleepy, sensual embrace. Babs' Jamaican accent came through a mouthful of Annabel's aristocratic breast: "Come to bed, Apples, we need you."

I went to the wardrobe and pulled out a shirt. "I have to go to a hospital."

Annabel sat up. "What is it?"

"Jane OD-ed on horse."

The sensuality drained from the two women. They had never met Jane, but they knew about her. And they knew how I would feel—the three of us were that close. Babs sat up on the edge of the bed.

I put on a suit, and, as an afterthought, a tie. I pocketed my keys and embraced Babs and Annabel. I stood with them for a moment, my eyes closed, drawing strength from their love as I had done before.

CHAPTER TWO

The grey interior of the elevator looked blankly at me as it dropped 40 flights. As I left the block a light London drizzle started, deepening my depression. I walked up the road to my car, wishing I had put on a coat.

I didn't get my usual kick from hearing the Jaguar's 12 cylinders hum effortlessly into life. I drove fast through the streets as the morning traffic began to build, giving myself a makeshift shave with the battery razor I kept in the glove box. When I switched the shaver off I could hear an inanely cheerful disc jockey on the radio. I turned him off.

I parked on a yellow line and hurried into the dark Victorian building of the hospital. The place was a maze of corridors with walls painted public-convenience green and dozens of anonymous doors.

I found a ward sister who told me I had better see the doctor. I smoked and kicked at chairs in the ante-room for ten minutes while she was away. There was a pile of very old copies of Practical Electronics on a table.

The doctor was a tall, tired Asian with a bald head. "Mr. Carstairs? I am Dr. Maya." We shook hands. "Your daughter is very ill, Mr. Carstairs. She injected herself with heroin. We don't know whether she will pull through—and if she does, it will be a long time before she is back to normal."

All that I knew already. "Can I see her?"

"No. She is in an intensive care unit. She is unconscious, so you could not speak to her anyway. But you may look through a window."

"I'll settle for that."

We walked along more green corridors and came to a door with a small glass panel in it. I looked through. All I could see was a dark head on a pillow. I turned away.

"Thank you, doctor."

He said: "Would you give your address and telephone number to the sister?"

"Sure." I found the ante-room again and gave the sister three phone numbers: the flat, the office and my car. As I was leaving I had a thought. I turned back to the sister and said: "Would you give me the address she was brought from?"

"Certainly," she said, looking through a file. She wrote it down for me and I left. I passed through the wrought-iron hospital gates and started walking. I wanted to think—something was boiling away at the back of my mind and I had to let it come out gradually. The hospital was in an old part of London, where disused warehouses and old railway arches rubbed shoulders with ugly concrete office blocks. The planners obviously had despaired of the place.

12

It was raining steadily now, and rain-coated commuters were scurrying about. I turned up the collar of my jacket and tried to keep close to the wall. My mood of helpless remorse was changing, although I did not know why. I wondered what had happened to Jane, that she had got in such a mess. No doubt she had got into bad company. I recognised that thought as a classic parental cliche, and gave a disgusted grunt. A passer-by looked startled.

Crying over spilt milk is not in my nature. My reaction is to curse, wipe up the mess, and make damn sure it doesn't happen again. I began to think about drugs. I had no hard convictions about them. In my flat was a large, expensive cube of Moroccan Gold which I took occasional shavings from. I couldn't be sure smoking pot was harmless, but I was certain it was less dangerous than whisky. Heroin was something else. It turned people into corpses.

I saw a cafe where people were buying tea and coffee in little paper cups to take with them into their offices. I went in and sat at a table. I was feeling taut and angry now, like a pulled bowstring without an arrow. The cafe proprietor was working like a machine behind the counter, filling cups with liquid, snapping on the plastic lids, taking money and giving change. He was supplying what people wanted, and the faster he supplied it the more money he made.

Just like the man——whoever he was——who was supplying the heroin that turned youngsters into corpses, I thought idly. And then the elusive thought which had been simmering in my subconscious burst like a Molotov cocktail in my head. I would find that bastard. And I would kill him.

CHAPTER THREE

The decision lay cold and hard and vicious in the pit of my stomach. It was a familiar feeling, and I recalled moments when I had had it before. Early in my career I had a builders' merchant's business. One day a man came into the yard and asked me for £50 protection money. I paid him, and the next time he called a six-foot concrete lintel fell on him and broke his back.

When I got a bit bigger, I was building a council complex when I discovered a rival was trying to discredit my firm by bribing the people who supplied me with doors to hold up deliveries. I bought a door-manufacturing firm, cut the prices, and took away all my supplier's customers. It took me six months to bankrupt him, then I put the prices up again.

A waitress came, and I ordered a fighting breakfast. As I sipped a mug of sweet tea I realised why I had asked the hospital sister for the address they had brought Jane from. I took out the piece of paper and looked at it again. It was a street in Islington.

I wolfed a meal my doctor would have frowned at—hot greasy bacon, sausages, fried eggs, and buttered toast. I had very little idea of how I would go about finding Mr. H.—the man at the head of the

14

heroin business. I could only plan as far ahead as my next step. That would have to do.

I paid my bill and hurried back to the car. The rain had brought out the London motorists in their frantic thousands, and the traffic moved desperately slowly. I picked up the car phone and called my secretary.

"I won't be in today, and possibly not for a few days," I told her. "Got your pad?"

"Yes."

"Tell John he's got a free hand with the negotiations for the Bayswater property, but there's a case of Scotch for him if he can get it for under £50,000. Tell Richard Elliott I've decided to go ahead with the French deal, and he can start drawing up contracts. Carstairs Construction wants that Gas Board contract, but I hear Pullman & Wilson are keen, so tell Bright he needs to shave a quarter of a million off the tender. Can you think of anything else?"

"There's a summons here for you from the Sussex police for speeding. Do you want me to do anything about that?"

"Plead guilty by post. You can sign my name. That all?"

"Yes."

I hung up and concentrated on struggling with the traffic. It had begun to clear when I got to Islington, and I soon found the street I was looking for.

It was a wide road with tall terraced houses that had long ago lost their air of middle-class gentility. They had three stories and a basement, and one or two had been modernized and tarted up, but the

15

place I pulled up outside looked about to fall over.

There was no answer when I knocked on the door. I waited a couple of minutes, then went down the steps to the basement. It was ankle-deep in decaying rubbish, and I had to pick my way around a couple of overflowing dustbins to get at the open window. I climbed in.

The place stank. There were empty bottles of cheap wine all over the filthy floor, and where the walls were not covered with posters and graffitti I could see peeling, damp-stained wallpaper. The furniture was all battered and very old, except for a superb hi-fi, a record spinning silently on the turntable where no one had bothered to lift the needle after the music stopped.

There were about a dozen prone bodies in the room, on mattresses and on the floor. In a corner, a girl wearing only a pair of green silk trousers opened one eye. I knelt beside her and asked in a low voice: "Do you know Jane Carstairs?"

She pointed to the other side of the room where there was what looked like a pile of old clothes. "She's his girl," she said, and went back to sleep. It must have been quite a party, I thought.

The pile of old clothes turned out to be a boy and a girl wrapped in a trench coat, asleep. I bent down and shook the fellow. He had long dark hair and a Zapata moustache like mine—only mine was grey. He probably thought Jane had gone off somewhere during the party—if he knew she was in hospital he would hardly be curled up so snugly with another girl already. I shook him again.

He sat up and brushed the hair out of his eyes. "What the fuck?" he groaned.

"Do you know Jane Carstairs?" I asked him.

"Gone to hospital," he muttered, and lay down again. That did it. I kicked him.

He yelled: "Look, you big creep, fuck off!"

The girl shushed him without opening her eyes. None of the other sleeping bodies stirred. I kicked the fellow again, harder.

He scrambled to his feet and stumbled over his jeans, which were around his ankles. I hit him twice, once with each fist, in the pit of the belly, and caught him over my shoulder as he fell. I might be out of condition, I thought, but I haven't forgotten what I learned about boxing in the Army.

I carried him up the stairs and out of the front door. He was still winded, fighting for his breath, when I lifted the lid of the Jaguar boot, dumped him inside, and slammed it shut. Then I got behind the wheel and drove fast, hitting all the bumps and potholes, to the canal.

I parked at a deserted spot. On one side of the road was a demolition site, and on the other was the canal. The air was damp and smelled bad. I opened the boot and hauled out the terrified boy.

I shoved him roughly up against the side of the car and took hold of his right ear in my left hand, a painful trick I learned from a sadistic schoolmaster. "Now talk to me," I said. "What are you to Jane?"

His resistance had completely dissolved. "I live with her," he said. "I met her three months ago, and moved into her pad. Her head is in the same place as mine, you know, and we can like talk. I like her, you know, is that a crime?"

"What does she do for a living?"

"Nothing much, but she calls herself an actress.

17

Well she's been in some blue films, that's all. I was supposed to be in them, but I . . . well, I couldn't get it up for the camera so another guy did it, but she shares the bread with me. And she's got a rich old man somewhere. She says he's a fucking capitalist, but she takes his money. In fact I don't think she needed the money for the films, but she's always doing crazy things. You know these mixed-up rich chicks."

"No," I said bitterly, "but you obviously do." I was learning the hard way. "What sort of stuff was she using?" I asked.

"Any fucking thing, man. When I met her she was shooting speed, then she started sniffing coke. We dropped some acid once but she had a really bad trip and it lasted two days. She thought I wanted to eat her, and she kept imagining that her body would still hurt while it was being chewed inside my guts and oh, man, was it a bad trip."

"Last night she OD-ed. It was horse. Where did she get the stuff?"

He looked at me suspiciously then. As his panic was subsiding, he was beginning to wonder why I was asking him these questions.

"A dealer called Harry Hat called. He's a spade, always wears wild hats. He is the big connection around here. What are you, the filth?"

I ignored his question. I had learned what I wanted to know, and a lot more I hadn't wanted to be told. But I had one more thing to ask.

"Was it her first heroin fix last night?"

"No, she's been on it a while now."

"Who turned her on to it?"

"I dunno."

He was getting cockier now. I brought my knee sharply up into his groin and punched his face for good measure. "You've been living with her for three months, you must know, you evil little bastard."

"Fuck it, I did, but you'll never prove it in court."

I didn't want to prove it in court. I threw him in the canal and walked away.

CHAPTER FOUR

When I got home I took off my clothes and went into the bathroom. Our bath was big enough for three—by design—and I always felt lonely in it on my own, so I opted for the shower. My metabolism began to slow down as the hot water massaged me, and by the time I had dried and put on a robe I had relaxed.

Babs had gone to work. She was a social worker in Lewisham, and I supposed she had decided some of her clients had worse problems than I did. I expect she was right. Besides, her job was important to her—if she hadn't been living with me she would have needed the money.

Annabel was slopping around the flat in an old dress that was literally in tatters. She was glad of any excuse to stay home from the studio where she worked—or said she worked: ten to one she spent more time screwing than sculpting. She was sexually ravenous. I had met her at a pop festival where she had been turned on by some rutting music from Rory Gallagher, and she had raped me. We did it standing up in the middle of a crowd of twenty thousand people and nobody noticed.

A few hours later at dawn, when most of the fans were sleeping, I had come across Annabel again. She was in a sleeping bag, beside a beautiful black girl. We made love again, and when it was over we realised the black girl had been watching. That was when Annabel introduced me to Babs.

They were lovers long before I met them, but their relationship was an uneven one. Annabel was enough for Babs, but Babs was not enough for Annabel. To complicate matters Annabel was bisexual and Babs was a straightforward lesbian.

At the festival they were on the point of splitting, because Annabel's other affairs made Babs insecure. But Babs got a kick out of watching me and Annabel, and she quickly became bisexual. They both moved in with me.

The psychology of the arrangement was pretty simple. Annabel's lusts were pretty well satisfied by me and Babs. Babs got the emotional security she needed, and I was just plain flattered to hell.

Now I sat down beside Annabel on a vast, amorphous sack of foam rubber we used as a couch. I lifted her dress and kissed her belly. She had nothing on underneath. She pushed my head lower, and I kissed the soft hair of her pubis briefly then pulled away.

She leaned over to the tray on the carpet and

poured tea into two bone china cups. "Want a lift in it?" she asked. I nodded. She poured a liberal dose of Scotch into the black tea. Then she lit two cigarettes and put one in my mouth. I drew on it and sipped the spiked tea. The tight knot of anger in my stomach had gone, leaving my mind clear.

I looked around me. The vast white space of my living room was dotted with bits of space-age furniture, mostly stuff Annabel had made and been unable to sell. One wall was covered with bookshelves and a hi-fi complex including a small portable television. Another wall was almost all glass, with a view of the river.

It looked like the home of a rich middle-aged trendy, which I supposed it was. But now it gave me no pleasure. My daughter was dying, and all my winning dynamism could not save her.

Reading my mind, Annabel said: "How was she?"

"No change."

"You were there a long time."

"No. I went somewhere else. I had a chat with the lad who turned her on."

"I hope you didn't . . . "

"No, I didn't kill him. I threw him in a canal. I expect he could swim. I didn't ask." I emptied the tea cup and poured some more. "He's a bastard, but a small-time one. I'm going after his boss."

Annabel sighed. "Apples, what the hell good will it do?"

"Look around you," I told her. "At the age of forty-three, what am I? Rich and powerful, a notorious winner, a man who has everything. Because he decides what he wants and goes all out to

21

get it. Well now I want something. A man's head on a platter. Because the man is evil, and he harmed someone I love. That's reason enough."

I put the cups on the tray and carried it out to the kitchen. As I washed up, ideas were coming and going in my head. I got dressed again, in navy flared trousers, a matching navy shirt, and a pale blue jacket. By the time I was ready to go out, I had decided what to do.

Outside the rain had stopped and the sun was doing its best to be cheerful. It was just after noon, and the traffic was still as thick as rhubarb jam. I hailed a cruising taxi and gave the driver the name of a pub near New Scotland Yard.

We were held up by some wretched procession in St. James's Park. The cabbie told me that the head of an African state was visiting. "Some jumped-up witch doctor comes to tea with the Queen and half London is paralysed by it," he said disgustedly.

"Yes," I said absent-mindedly. There were times when I had the patience to argue with bigots, and this was not one of them.

He was an old cabbie, so he knew the pub. Many wouldn't have. It was hidden down a narrow alley-way which looked like the driveway of a building unless you were in the know. And anyone who had stumbled across it accidentally would hardly have been lured inside by appearance of the place.

During my rather brief career as a crime reporter I had spent many lunch hours in that pub. It was used almost exclusively by CID, and it never closed unless it was empty. Lunch hour generally ended around teatime.

I walked up to the bar and ordered a Scotch. The

barman was a sour-faced Scot who never touched a drop. As he poured I said: "Don't you remember me?"

He replied: "How do you think I knew you wanted ice and soda?"

I looked at the drink. Sure enough, he had made it just as I liked it—lots of ice, and fifty-fifty with soda. I smiled and extended my hand over the bar. "How are you, Jock?"

He shook my hand. "It's good to see you, boy," he said, looking about as cheerful as a bloodhound with mumps. But it was nice to be called "boy".

"How's business?" I asked him.

"Usual crowd of ruffians in here," he replied.

"Any of the old bunch from the Drugs Squad still come in here?"

"Some. Of course, old Nellie Nelson's been drinking in the Crown since they made him Chief-bloody-Superintendent. But Bert Payne comes in here, causing trouble. And your big buddy Arthur. They made him up to D.I. I can't think why, he never had any brains."

"I'll say he didn't. Remember that car he bought from a grass?" The conversation went on that way for a couple more double Scotches, then Detective-Inspector Arthur Lambourne arrived.

I hardly recognized him. Instead of his old charcoal grey suit with white shirt and navy tie, he wore a trendy herringbone three-piece suit with a sunburst kipper tie and matching breast pocket handkerchief. His hair was earlobe length, and he looked prosperous.

"Jesus, you've changed!" I told him. "You aren't even wearing braces. How are the villains supposed

23

to recognise a flatfoot if they dress like that?"

"Hello, Apples," he said with a smile. "If you're buying I'll have a large Scotch, a pint of lager, and a ham sandwich."

"A half of shandy for my friend, Jock, if you will," I said.

Jock drew a pint of draught Guinness, which Arthur always drank.

"Caught any villains lately?" I asked Arthur.

"Pot party here and there, you know. Nothing spectacular."

"You haven't done badly, Detective-Inspector."

"But you've done better, from what I hear. How do you make all that money? Is it legit?"

"Mostly." I laughed. "I buy and sell property, sometimes build on it. I own some magazines that bring in a shekel or two."

"You're coining it, my mate. I read the financial pages. So what do you want that you come to this old dump and buy me a drink?"

I laughed, but there was an edge in his voice that told me he was being wary. He was entitled to be, I thought.

"What I always wanted when I bought you drinks. Information."

"For one of your magazines?"

"No, they're not in that line. This is personal."

"Well the worst I can say is I don't know. Shoot."

"Ever come across a black man called Harry Hat? I believe he's a pusher."

"Yes, we know him. Deals in heroin, cocaine, mainly. He's small fry. We could have him if we really tried, but he's small fry. If we worked on every nasty little dealer we know of, we'd have no

24

men left to go after the big fish. Why do you want to know?"

"I want a word with him. Like I said, it's personal. Where can he be found?"

"There's a club called the Purple End near Leicester Square. Not very swank, but not exactly a dump either. One of these days we'll raid it. What do you want to talk to him about?"

"I think he may be able to assist me with my inquiries." Arthur laughed. "If he tells me anything that might help you, I'll pass it on," I added.

Arthur did not want to leave it there, but at that moment there was a raucous shout.

"Hey, it's Apples Carstairs, the man who called the Assistant Commissioner a sergeant!" That was a reference to an early error of mine which incredibly had got into the paper. I turned to see three more of the old crowd. I bought a round of drinks, then someone bought another. We talked about old times, and I bought several more rounds.

At four o'clock I crawled out of the place and fell into a cab. When I got home I lay down and slept. Heavily.

CHAPTER FIVE

I woke up at nine o'clock. I took a shower to clear my head of whisky fumes. It didn't work. I dressed in plimsolls, loon pants and a T-shirt with a hammer and sickle on the front.

Annabel was out and Babs was in the kitchen. I mixed a Bloody Mary and swallowed it in one. That worked. I threw two steaks into the frying pan.

"Hello, Babs," I said.

"Welcome back to the land of the living," she said, and kissed my cheek.

I hunted around in the fridge for some frozen vegetables. "Want to go dancing?" I asked her.

"I'd like to, but what about your bad back?"

"Insolent youth," I said, and tried to wallop her backside. She dodged me and ran out of the kitchen.

I caught her in the middle of the living room and brought her down with a flying tackle. We landed in a helplessly giggling heap on a giant cushion. I got on top and sat on her back, facing her feet. I lifted her skirt.

"I'll show you how bad my back is," I said.

I pushed her knickers down and slapped her small brown backside. She gave a squeal of mock fear. But her rear was really too nice to hurt, and besides we weren't into the spanking kick. So I kissed it instead. Her skin was so deliciously soft on my lips that I kept on kissing for a while. Then I gently bit her. She moved her hips slowly up and down, and spread her legs slightly.

My head went lower until my face was brushing the inside of her thigh. We had stopped laughing now.

Suddenly I took hold of her hips and rolled over on to my back, pulling her with me. She sat up, her legs astride my face. I buried my face in her loins. She was panting hard now, and so would I if I had been able to breathe. She took my head in her hands and pressed my face more deeply into her, moving her pelvis compulsively up and down. My head began to sing. "Now," I breathed.

She wriggled back along the carpet, still on her knees, until her pelvis was above mine. Then she lowered herself, guiding me inside her with one expert brown hand.

"Keep still," she whispered.

Then she moved up and down, and side to side, with me completely still inside her. Her internal muscles gripped me with incredible sensations, and the tension built up unbearably, like static electricity on my skin, until I longed to thrust at her. I watched her small breasts jiggle up and down as she moved faster. Sweat broke out all over her slender body, and a rivulet ran down from her neck, between her breasts, and across her belly.

I sat up and took one swollen black nipple between my lips. She crushed my head to her chest, and I sucked hard. Her legs curled around my waist. I could bear it no longer.

I stood up, with Babs clinging to me. Her arms went around my neck and I supported her with one hand under each hard buttock.

I lifted her, then thrust myself forward as I let her down. We moved faster and faster, until Babs shouted hoarsely: "Baby, baby, here it comes!" We came like a double bomb going off, a dynamite orgasm that seemed to shake the room. My legs turned to jelly and we collapsed on the floor.

After a while Babs lifted her head from my belly and said: "I guess your back is O.K."

I smiled contentedly. I like flattery. Then I sniffed. "What's burning?"

27

She laughed. "My vagina."

I leapt to my feet and ran into the kitchen. The steaks were on fire. I lifted the smoking pan from the cooker and dumped it in the sink, cursing away to myself. Babs came to the kitchen door.

"Look what I've done," I said disgustedly. She leaned against the doorpost and started to laugh.

"What's so funny?" I said, a bit testily.

She laughed all the more. "You, naked from the waist down, standing there with a burnt frying pan in your hand . . . " I laughed then. I must have looked pretty undignified.

I found another frying pan, got two more steaks out of the freezer, and started again.

The doorman charged me a fiver for the pair of us. I guessed that was about twice the normal entrance fee for the Purple End, but it served us right for looking affluent. Babs was stunning in tight yellow trousers with bottoms like tents, and a miniature halter top. I wore a T-shirt, but I had some fancy jewellery on.

The way in was like the entrance to a dungeon. We had to walk down a steep, narrow concrete stair which could not possibly have passed any fire regulations. At the bottom was a double door which led to the club.

Inside, everything was purple—floor, walls, tables, chairs, and even the tits of the topless waitresses.

On stage a five-piece rock band, all dressed in purple, was making a very loud noise and being completely ignored by the clientele. A few people

28

were dancing in a desultory fashion on the postage-stamp dance floor.

We found a table. A waitress came and dangled her purple boobs under my nose. Two watery whiskies cost two quid. The band went off and a disc-jockey started playing records. He put on very long L.P. tracks, probably because it meant less work for him.

An old Cream number came on and woke me from the near-slumber induced by the club. I took Babs' hand. "Let's dance," I said.

It was fun for a while, but the standard of the music swiftly dropped. The DJ ran to a taste in avant-garde German rock, and the man who can dance to that would jive to Stockhausen. We sat down again and had two more diluted Scotches.

"What an awful place this is," Babs said finally.

"This is swinging London," I told her.

"Apples, why are we here?"

"To see how the other half live."

"C'mon, honey, I want to know."

"There is a man here I want to see."

"What sort of a man?"

"A spade who wears fancy hats and sells heroin to kids."

She nodded and leaned back in her chair, a troubled expression on her face. Annabel had no doubt explained to her what I was planning. I could see she wanted to say Don't do it, forget it, let's go home. But we had an unspoken agreement that we didn't try to run one another's lives. She kept silent.

Then I saw him at the bar. He was tall, with a beard and sparse moustache, and looked very, very cool. He wore black leather trousers, platform shoes, and a beautiful cream shirt which clung to his narrow torso as tightly as a suntan. But the clincher was a pink Stetson with a black hat band. It couldn't be anyone but Harry Hat.

I stood up. "I won't be a minute," I told Babs. She bit her lip and nodded.

I strolled over to the bar and stood beside Harry Hat. He was sipping a long rum drink. He took a packet of Chesterfield 100's out of his hat band and flipped one into his mouth. I struck a match and held it out.

He turned away, took a miniature lighter from his trouser pocket, and lit his cigarette.

"Harry," I said.

He leaned against the bar and blew smoke out into the smog that already filled the place. Without looking at me he said lightly: "Fuck off, grandpa."

I persisted. "Want to do some business?"

He looked at me then. "O.K." he said in the same I-don't-really-give-a-shit tone of voice. He walked away. I followed him.

He led me through a door beside the bar into a damp concrete corridor. A few yards along he opened a door marked Office and walked in. As I passed through the doorway something hard came from nowhere and hit me behind the ear. I whipped around and took a blow to the belly. A stick hit the back of my head.

Suddenly I was on the floor, an agonising rain of blows hitting my head, belly, groin. A blur of emotionless faces revolved in front of my eyes, and I saw hands holding hammers, bottles, ashtrays. Just before I blacked out I saw Harry Hat's face again, his ridiculous Stetson still on his head, just like a cowboy in a B-grade Western. It was my last agonized thought.

When I came to it was dark and cold. I was lying on rough ground, and something sticky covered my left eye. I tried to get up, and my body screamed its refusal.

As sensation returned I discovered I was a mass of spots of pain which gradually blurred into one massive ache. I lay still for an age, summoning up strength. At last I got to my feet.

I leaned on a drainpipe. I was in a yard full of garbage. Distant music told me I was not far from the Purple End.

I took a step forward, stumbled into a dustbin, and fell down again. But my will-power was returning now, and I gritted my teeth against the pain and stood up again. Ahead of me I could see a patch of light grey in the darkness, and I made for it.

I staggered down an alleyway, and kept going until suddenly I found myself in the bright lights of Leicester Square. I leaned against a wall. Passers-by gave me a wide berth and pretended not to look at me. They probably took me for an alky, but a policeman might get suspicious, and I didn't feel like inventing explanations.

I figured out which direction the car was in and moved on. In two minutes I found it and fell behind the wheel. I sat there, resting. There was a small sound from the back seat. I turned quickly.

It was Babs. I almost wept. Her halter top was gone, her trousers were torn and dirty, and her face and chest were cut and bruised.

"Apples?" she said in a terrified voice.

My voice cracked. "What happened?"

31

"After you went . . . they asked me to go into the office. Said you wanted me . . . then they raped me." She sobbed. "Three times."

"Jesus, no." I buried my face in my hands.

CHAPTER SIX

I called my doctor on the car phone. When we got to the door of the flat she was waiting outside. She was a greying divorcee in her fifties, and from what I had heard one of the original Women's Libbers. She was also not on the National Health, which was why she got there so fast.

I told her to see to Babs first.

"You look worse," she told me.

"Not to me I don't. Besides, it was my fault."

With that she didn't argue. She began to clean Babs up and bandage her, while I started some coffee. I was feeling bitter remorse for the second time that day. Babs had been raped before, by her father, which was probably part of the reason she had been a lesbian. Now I had taken her right into danger and it had happened again. Did everyone I touched have to be hurt?

The doctor tucked Babs up in bed and started on me. She ran an expert eye over my bruised body and said: "I've been around a while, Mr. Carstairs, and I can see that you have been professionally beaten up."

"Very perceptive," I said sarcastically.

She ignored the insult. "Are you going to the police?"

"No. Are you?"

She shook her head. "But what about Barbara?"

"No again."

"Why?"

"I've seen too many rape cases in court. There are always more men than women on the jury. The man tells a tale of being led on, and they acquit. I'll save Babs the embarrassment."

"And yourself," she said pointedly. It was a dart that went home. I shut up.

When she had fixed me up she said: "Is there any point in my telling you to rest for a couple of days?"

"No."

"Then at least make sure Barbara does."

I looked her in the eye. "I will do that," I promised. She closed her case and saw herself out.

I poured two cups of coffee, added a hefty brandy to each, and took one in to the bedroom. Babs got up on one elbow and took the cup.

"I really fouled things up," I said.

She knew that already. "Yes," she said.

"I'm sorry." She knew that too. I wanted her to forgive me, and say she still loved me. I wanted to kneel beside her and beg forgiveness, but I knew she would despise that kind of emotional blackmail. Come to that, so would I.

I realised she was not going to say anything. She was not going to let me off the hook, and I didn't deserve it. As to whether she still loved me, she was probably thinking about it very hard. I left her.

As I was closing the bedroom door she called: "I

know you didn't mean it to happen, Apples."

"But I should have foreseen it," I said bitterly, half to myself. If she heard she did not reply. I closed the door softly.

I sat down gingerly and picked up my coffee. Carstairs the cunt, I thought, always taking problems like a bull at a gate. It was in Stepney that I learned to rush things, to act fast. My family had moved there when I was thirteen.

Most people think my Cockney accent is for real and my BBC English faked. In fact it's the other way around. I was born into a classy family which went bankrupt. When I switched from public school to an East End secondary school the first thing I learned was to talk like the other kids. Another useful tactic was to fight first and ask what it was all about afterwards.

The move to that little terraced house killed my father, but it grew me up—not that I'd wish it on anyone else, all the same. It was there that I developed what I suppose you would call my philosophy of life. No, survival tactics is what I developed.

Quick reactions and iron determination had served me well early on, but as I became a big businessman I had to learn other techniques. I had had to train myself to pause, evaluate, and think ahead. I thought I had the old Carstairs well under control. But he had reared his ugly head during this latest crisis.

All right, I told myself, treat this thing like a business deal. Figure out the angles, look for the opening, grab the percentage, and keep the back door open for a quick pull-out.

I wanted to find Mr. H., the man who ferried heroin into London. I had tried starting from the bottom of his organisation. Jane's boy friend had led me to Harry Hat, and the trail had stopped there. Painfully.

Somehow they had been expecting me—I had yet to figure out how they knew. But whatever the explanation, they had been one step ahead of me and I had fouled up that approach.

I was stuck, without a single useful contact, with my only lead gone very sour on me. All I had was money and power—in another world. The world where I was a big man, where a word from me moved financial mountains, might have been in another galaxy a million light-years from the world of Harry Hat and Mr. H. Somehow I had to use my strengths in that world. I had to use my brains and my wealth, instead of my fists, which were flabby from years of disuse.

Use money instead of fists, go in from the top instead of the bottom . . . Suddenly ideas started coming. Half a dozen schemes came in and out of my head in a few seconds. The old Carstairs cranium was in gear. I pulled my desk out of the wall and started scribbling notes.

When Annabel arrived home the brandy bottle was almost empty, the ashtray overflowed, and I had a plan.

I turned around in my chair. "Something's happened," I said.

"That I can see." Her high forehead creased in a concerned frown.

"I went after Harry Hat, the horse dealer. He was expecting me."

35

She kissed my battered face.

I said: "You haven't heard the worst. I took Babs. She got raped."

Annabel drew back from me in horror. Her eyes flashed anger. "You fucking cretin!" she blazed. For a moment it looked as if she was going to hit me, but she changed her mind and strode into the bedroom. I heard low voices for a while, and then I heard Annabel sobbing.

I put on my shoes and jacket and went out. I would hardly be welcome in bed—and I had work to do.

It was four a.m. when I drew up outside a small house in Chelsea. It was a tiny place, but detached, and worth a great deal of money. I could see lights behind curtained windows, which meant there was a party on. There was almost every night.

I almost could have been walking up the path to a select country cottage—until I opened the unlocked door. A blast of music and hot, smoky air hit me. I closed the door behind me quickly to spare the neighbours.

"Chadwell, darling!" said a man's voice.

Yes, Chadwell is my name. I never let on to it in Stepney—told everyone my name was Carstairs and refused to give my Christian name. And since the rhyming slang for stairs is apples and pears, I got called Apples. Somehow Alastair John had found out about Chadwell, and he thought it was simply lovely, darling, and he was the only person in the world who used it.

He came up to me now, dressed in a floor-length kaftan and with his face made up expertly. He kissed me. I kissed him back. Well, it gave him a thrill and it cost me nothing—besides, I wanted a favour.

"Darling, don't tell me you've been converted," he said in surprise. He spoke in a high sing-song, because he always camped it up for my benefit.

"When that happens you'll be the first to know, Al."

"Well, it's not like you to run out of dope in the middle of the night."

"I haven't come to buy any of your low-grade hash, either." He was my local supplier.

"Well, come and be tempted, anyway." In case the message isn't clear yet, he was as queer as a five-bob note. He took me possessively by the arm and walked me across the room.

The place was packed with extravagantly-dressed people of all sexes, dancing, drinking, talking, making love. A few were playing Monopoly in a corner—no doubt they had introduced some kinky twist to it. The light in the room was a kind of gold colour, which made everyone look even weirder. The music was David Bowie—who else?—and very loud.

Alastair handed me a strange-looking concoction in a glass. I sipped it. It was ice-cold, and tasted of vodka and strawberries. "Delicious," I told him.

A man came up and batted his false eyelashes at me. "Well hello," he said.

"Go away, Stuart," said Alastair.

"Keeping him for yourself, Alastair?" said the man with a leer.

"Keeping him away from the likes of you,

anyway." The man drifted off. We sat on the floor.

"So you haven't become AC-DC yet, despite the influence of your two charming flatmates," said Alastair. He never gave up hope of corrupting me.

"I envy you bisexuals," I said. "You must have twice the fun. But for me it doesn't work."

There were three people on the floor just in front of us in a contorted mutual embrace. As I tried to figure out who was doing what to whom, two more joined them. I looked on interestedly.

"Did you come to watch?" asked Alastair.

"That neither," I said. I tore my attention away from the growing pile of bodies on the floor. "I want to ask you one question about the topic you are most expert on."

"Sex?"

"Drugs."

"Chadwell, you're being a bitch."

"I mean it." A hand emerged from the pile of bodies and started to stroke me. I couldn't tell whether it was male or female, and besides, it was a chancy business to get involved in one of Alastair's orgies. I removed the wandering paw.

"All right, Chadwell, what is this burning question? Is pot an aphrodisiac? Does coke make you impotent? Is a pepped-up teenybopper a good lay?"

"Wrong, wrong, and wrong again. How can you be so decadent?"

"Flatterer."

The room began to spin slightly. I realized I must have been drinking pretty steadily for almost twenty-four hours. I decided I had better get this over with.

"Alastair, if you wanted to buy a million pounds worth of heroin, where would you go?"

"What kind of a silly question is that? No one in London would be fool enough to hold that much—even if they had the capital. And anyway, you know I'm strictly in the soft drugs business."

"I'm serious, Al. And I didn't say it had to be London."

He looked at me. "Precious arseholes, I believe the dear fellow means it. The answer's Marseilles, of course—but you must be out of your mind. A million pounds—Apples, I have a horrid feeling you're serious."

"Thank you, mate." I got to my feet without too much difficulty, and negotiated the writhing heap of bodies which now contained almost everyone in the room. I looked back as I opened the door. Alastair was still sitting on the floor, looking into his drink with a frown, and shaking his peroxided head slowly from side to side.

CHAPTER SEVEN

The fresh air outside hit me like a bucketful of cold water. I leaned against the closed door until the street firmed up, then made as straight a line as I could to the car.

It was a good job I did not have far to go to the

flat. I didn't see a single traffic light on the way home, and I know there are about half a dozen. The streets were deserted.

I double-parked outside the flat and went in. In the bedroom a small lamp was on, but both the girls were asleep: Annabel lying on her back snoring, and Babs with her head on Annabel's chest. I looked away.

I packed a sober bottle-green suit, a plain silk tie the same colour, and an eggshell-green shirt. I added some T-shirts and underwear and a towel, then found my passport and threw that into the suitcase. I took off my clothes and put on denim jeans, plimsolls, and a Levi jacket.

I stuffed cigarettes and money into the pocket of the jacket and made some coffee. While it was perking I wrote a note to the girls. On it I put: I may be away for a few days. I love you both. Apples.

I poured the coffee into a vacuum flask, swallowed what was left over, and went back down to the car.

Driving to Dover I felt more cheerful than I had done all the previous day. Dawn was breaking as I left South London, and I opened the window for the morning air to clear my head of alcohol. The XJ12 was going very sweetly, but I kept her down to 100 m.p.h. as I didn't feel like tearing about. Bowling along the A2 with a Gauloise in my gob and the Beatles blasting out of the stero tapedeck, with not another car in sight, I felt at peace with the world.

Naturally, I got stopped for speeding by the police.

I hadn't even seen them in my mirror until the old siren started up. We pulled over on to the hard shoulder, and they got out, looking very stern.

"Where's the fire?" said one. I wondered how many times he had said that. But I was very sweet to them, as I was terrified of being breathalysed. That would really snarl things up.

"I'm sorry, officer. I just didn't realise my speed had crept up."

"Hurt your face, have you?" said the other, looking at my bruises.

"I had an argument with a pavement," I said.

They took down my name and address at a leisurely pace, then pushed off. I followed them at dead-on 70 m.p.h. until they turned off the road. Then I upped my speed to 130. Lightning never strikes in the same place twice.

I found the best hotel in Dover and went in for breakfast. I ordered a whole grapefruit, a bowl of porridge, bacon and three eggs, a pot of coffee, and a lot of toast. As I smoked and finished the coffee, the hangover hit. My head ached, and I felt weak and helpless. After the last twenty-four hours, I supposed I was entitled to be.

From the lobby I telephoned the hospital. There was no change in Jane's condition.

I read a paper until the banks opened, and went in to get some francs. Then I drove on to the car ferry.

It was a rough crossing. Everyone was seasick except me. I slept like a log the whole way.

I took things very easy driving down through France. I stopped at lunchtime for an incredibly good meal at a country restaurant, although I laid off the wine and drank mineral water instead.

Driving through France is marvellous if you aren't in a hurry. The roads are straight and not too crowded, and the flat land lets you see the countryside for miles around. There are no hedges to spoil the view, as there are in English country lanes.

As I got back on the road after lunch I saw a tall bearded fellow in jeans thumbing beside the road, and picked him up. He was a drop-out from Boston, U.S.A., bumming his way around the world.

After a while I told him to choose a tape. He picked Stevie Wonder's Music of My Mind. I began to like him.

"What did you do before you dropped out?" I asked.

"I had my own advertising agency in Massachusetts," he said. "I bought it for a song after I finished business school, spent three years of my life building it up, then sold it for a hundred thousand dollars."

"Why?"

"I realised I didn't like it. And I didn't like advertising. It takes away people's freedom to decide for themselves."

"Does it?"

"Sure. Advertising is how American businessmen control the American people. And that's not just my theory—that's what they teach you in business school. I tell you, in the brainwashing field we are so far ahead of the Russians."

I looked at him sideways. He was smiling—he meant what he said, but he wasn't too earnest about it. He had the kind of face people call pleasantly ugly—a great big nose, soft brown eyes, and long, clean hair.

"You mind if I roll a joint?" he asked.

"Go ahead," I said. An idea was forming in my mind as he took out an old tobacco tin from his jeans pocket. He sprinkled shredded tobacco on a giant-sized cigarette paper, then wrapped a small piece of resin in silver paper and scorched it with a match.

"What did you do with the hundred thousand dollars?" I asked him.

"Gave it back to the people it was stolen from," he said. He sprinkled the resin in the tobacco and rolled up the reefer. "I built houses and sold them at a loss."

"So you've got no money."

"When I need it I work." He twisted the end of the rolled cigarette and fired the paper. When the tobacco was alight he drew on it, held it down for a long moment, and exhaled.

"Open the quarter-light and flick the ash out of the window," I told him. I was thinking that he could be very useful to me. He looked tough, and he was intelligent. He was no stranger to the dope scene, and—most important of all—he was practically untraceable if the police ever got interested in my activities.

He passed me the joint. I took a draw. My hangover was passing now, and although I didn't normally mix drugs with alcohol, a couple of blasts wouldn't hurt.

"Got any plans for the next few days?" I asked him.

"Yes. Sunbathing, wine, and see if I can't score with a bronzed French chick."

"How would you like a few days of highly-paid work instead?"

"For you?"

"Yes."

"What are you doing?"

"Setting up a dope deal. How do you feel about heroin?"

"It's death, man. But each man has the right to choose his own death."

"So. Are you in? You get £1,000 for a week's work."

"Yes. I'm in." He took the last drag from the roach, looked out of the back window, and dropped the fag-end out of the window.

I was thinking. This simplified matters. As we reached the outskirts of Marseilles I gave him instructions.

"We'll check into different hotels tonight. Later on in the evening, you go into the town and score some horse. When you get to a dealer, tell him you have a friend who wants to set up a deal. A big one.

"Arrange to be at a fixed place—a cafe, say—at a certain time tomorrow morning, to meet the big guy."

"So I act as a buffer for you."

"At this stage, yes."

I dropped him off at a pension near the centre of town. I took the phone number, and left without telling him where I would be staying. "I'll call you in the morning, I said. Before I left I found out his name was Guy House. I didn't tell him mine.

I found a good hotel and checked in. I ate, showered, and went to bed. It was about time.

The bedside phone woke me. I had asked to be called at 7 a.m. I had only halfway caught up on my sleep, but I reckoned I would work for another day or so.

I ordered a pint of fresh orange juice and some coffee from room service, then dialled the place where Guy was staying.

"Pension Blanc," said a woman's voice.

"Monsieur House, s'il vous plait," I said in my appalling French.

"Un moment."

A few minutes later he came to the phone.

"How did you make out?" I asked him.

"Easy as falling off a log. The town is packed with pushers. You can't cross the street without being offered half a dozen kinds of dope, and it's dirt cheap. And the fuzz have either given up or got bribed."

"Good. Did you fix a meet?"

"Yeah. Man who sold me the horse sounded very keen—maybe he gets a commission. I'm meeting his supplier at the Cafe Pierre at eleven."

"Fine. The man you see there still won't be the No. One, so just repeat the message. And if you see me, don't notice me."

"Right."

I hung up and finished my liquid breakfast. I

didn't bother to shave, but dressed in my jeans and put on my sunglasses. Then I slipped out of the hotel.

First I hired an anonymous-looking little Renault and a map of the city. Then at 10:45 I parked near the Cafe Pierre.

Guy was sitting drinking wine at a pavement table. He did not look at me as I passed.

I went into the cafe and bought croissants, coffee, and *Le Monde*. I sat at the window where I could see Guy. The paper was full of a scandal about a pop singer, a politician's wife, and a pot party. Christ, I thought, everyone's at it.

At exactly eleven o'clock a man in a black suit and tie walked up to Guy and sat down. He had short oiled hair and pointed shoes. They shook hands and talked for a while.

Then Guy started to get a bit agitated. He was shaking his head determinedly, and the Frenchman seemed to be insisting on something.

Then the Frenchman stood up and put his hand in his jacket pocket. A black Citroen appeared from nowhere and pulled up at the kerb. I stood up and walked out of the cafe.

I passed between the car and the table just as Guy stood up. The Frenchman was behind him now, and seemed to be prodding him with the hand in his pocket.

The rear door of the car opened, and I could see there were two men in it. I walked on to my Renault.

As I opened the door I saw Guy and the Frenchman get into the Citroen. I pulled out into the traffic at the same time as they did.

Following the black car through the town centre was quite a feat. I managed to keep its high roof in sight most of the time, but I had to stay a couple of cars behind it to prevent the villains suspecting me. I almost lost it when a lorry got between us and the Citroen and did an unexpected right turn, and I did lose it at a set of traffic lights. But I guessed its direction right and caught up with it again.

It took a main highway out of the city and then turned off at a roundabout. A couple more turns and it was following a narrow country road, and now it was much more difficult for me to be inconspicuous.

But my goose was finally cooked when the Citroen got stuck behind a large lorry. I had no option but to pull right up behind it. They must by now suspect me of follwing them, I thought. So I decided to do the one thing a discreet car-follower would never do. I put my hand on my horn and pretended I wanted to pass.

I kept indicating, pulling over, pulling back and shaking my fist. The men in the Citroen ignored me and the lorry driver put his arm out his cab window and made an international gesture.

After about a mile the Citroen suddenly turned off the road into an almost-hidden drive. As I passed the entrance I caught a glimpse of a large white villa surrounded by trees.

I drove on about a mile and stopped. I looked at my map and figured out where I was, then marked the spot where the black car had pulled in. I worked out the quickest way back to the town centre without passing the villa, and drove on.

Back at the hotel, I altered my appearance. I shaved and put on my bottle-green suit and tie. Then I had a leisurely lunch.

They would be grilling Guy now, I thought as I ate. But they wouldn't get any information out of him. He didn't know my name, or where I could be found; whether I was on the level, whether I was working for someone, or whether I had any bully-boys with me.

Then they would start to get a little worried. They would wonder whether their action had put me off and lost them some business. They would get greedily curious about just how big a deal I wanted to pull off. They would start to worry that I might go to a rival firm—for there had to be more than one big heroin dealer in the world's H capital.

They would start to think about how they could find me. Then I would turn up on their doorstep.

CHAPTER EIGHT

After lunch I approached the head receptionist in the hotel lobby. He spoke perfect English, and understood even better the folded paper I pressed discreetly into his hand. Then I showed him my map.

"There is a large white villa on this road just

here," I told him. "It is just the kind of property I am looking for. Can you find out who owns it?"

"I can tell you now, sir," he said. "It belongs to a Monsieur Charles LeGrand. He is a businessman."

"Thank you," I said. The name sounded just like the kind of alias an egotistic French crook would use.

It was late afternoon when I purred up the drive of the villa in the Jag. The house was a vast white oblong dotted with shutters. The grounds were immaculately kept, and several flash cars were parked in front of the place.

A butler in his shirtsleeves answered the door. He was taller than me, and looked as if somebody had accidentally trodden on his face when he was a baby.

"Est-ce-que Monsieur LeGrand est chez lui?" I asked.

When he had got past my awful accent he said: "Non."

I took a chance and stepped past him into the house. "Lui dit que l'Anglais qu'il cherche est ici," I said haughtily. The man was clearly in two minds whether to hit me or do as I said. But effrontery paid off, and after an internal struggle he went off into the depths of the house.

I looked around me. The hall was fairly impressive, with white walls, a high ceiling, and a mosaic floor. I peeped into a room off it. I saw an Indian carpet, paintings on the walls, and dark furniture. It looked smart, but under-used.

The butler reappeared at the far end of the hall.

"Venez ici," he called. For manners this fellow was no Jeeves.

I followed him down a corridor into the bowels of the place. He led me into a back room.

The atmosphere stopped me in my tracks: cigar smoke, sweat, booze and dirt had all contributed to the smell. There were some battered armchairs on a once-good carpet now holed by fag ends. The centrepiece of the room was a card table around which a few thugs were gambling. One of them stood up.

"Monsieur LeGrand?" I asked.

"Well?" he said in English.

I got the picture. I was being treated like a rather unwelcome tradesman until I proved myself to be worth courtesy. I pressed on.

"I would like a word with you, Monsieur."

He said: "Before we go any further, Mister . . . "

I filled in: "Charlie Large." If he got the joke it didn't register. He went on: "Mr. Large, what is the size of this deal you want to make with me?"

"One hundred thousand pounds."

His manner changed fast. "All right. Follow me."

He led me through yet another corridor into one of the rooms obviously reserved for impressing people rather than living in. I sat down and studied the man as he poured drinks.

He was rather fat, about my age, with short white hair and a little white moustache. He wore braces and carpet slippers, and a small cigar dangled from his mouth. The cigar had gone out.

He looked like a grocer who through some stroke

of luck had become very rich. I supposed that was roughly what he was.

I decided that the way I had been treated when I arrived was not a careful insult, but simple bad manners. He handed me a drink.

I said: "Where is my colleague?"

"Ah, the American. He is here. I am afraid we were a little rough with him for a while, but he is not injured. It was clear he really knew nothing. Shall I send for him?"

"No. The less he knows, the better—for him and for me."

"Well, shall we get down to business?"

"Right. I want five hundred kilos of heroin. I must have it within a matter of days. I am not prepared to haggle with you over money. I will pay you the market price here, which is one hundred thousand English pounds." I was indebted to Guy for that last piece of information.

The grocer fired his cigar with a table lighter and frowned. "Your price is low, but it is a bulk order."

"Have we got a deal?"

"Not yet. You see—if I let you have that kind of quantity, it means other buyers will have to go without. Now, we cannot upset our big customers, the Americans. It would not only be bad business, but rather dangerous to our health." He gave a short laugh, but I could tell there was real fear behind it. "That means we would have to let down our other big market, London." He looked at me out of the corner of his eyes. "But then, perhaps that is what you want."

He was pretty sharp for a grocer. I gave a non-committal nod.

"Very well," he said. "I can deliver in seven days, barring unforeseen snags."

"Good. Where do I make the pick-up?"

"Here." He saw my raised eyebrows, and added: "The local police are on the payroll." He crossed his baggy-trousered legs and lit his cigar yet again. "Bring a car, and we see to the packing of the goods."

"How do you want to be paid?"

He thought for a minute. ".We normally insist on cash, but this is a very large amount. I will have to think about it."

I already had thought about it. "I have a suggestion," I said. "It would help me to cover my tracks if the payment could be made to look legitimate. I have a property company here in France, called Etats Anglais. If some kind of deal can be arranged through that company and one of your companies . . ." An operation the size of LeGrand's, which could supply £100,000 worth of heroin in seven days, had to have several front organisations.

"A good idea. We will see what can be arranged: and we will have something ready when we deliver the goods."

"Then, if you will send for my colleague, we will be on our way."

He got up and went out. I leaned back and sipped at the Scotch. It had been easier than I expected.

He returned in a couple of minutes with Guy at his side.

"It's about time," said Guy. "What kept you?" He had a black eye.

I stood up and shook hands with LeGrand. He saw us to the door.

In the car Guy leaned back and rubbed his stomach.

"They hurt you?" I asked.

"A little," he said. "Was that part of your plan?"

"No," I said. "I was playing it by ear. But it worked out all right."

He gave a disgusted grunt. I smiled. "Are you still in the game?"

"Yes, I'm still in."

I handed him a wad of notes. "There is the equivalent of about five thousand dollars there," I said. "I want you to go to Paris and buy a five-ton lorry in good condition. Also buy a consignment of something like dried milk, detergent, any white powder. Arrange legitimate export papers for the consignment. Load the goods on to the lorry and garage it. Then hire a small car and be back at Pension Blanc seven days from now."

"Got it," he said. I made him repeat it all the same.

Then I asked him: "Why are you in this?"

"You're paying me."

"Yes, but you don't need the kind of money you're getting from me. And if you did there must be easier ways to earn it."

He looked at the money in his hand. "Are you worried I'll run off with this?"

I laughed. "That's the least of the risks I'm taking."

"Forget it," he said. I pulled up outside his pension. "One reason I took this trip is for . . . well, adventure, I guess. But bumming around the world is just what it sounds like—bumming. Bumming lifts, food, money, cigarettes. In six months this is the nearest I've got to adventure."

"Is that all?"

He smiled and looked at me. "No, it's not. The rest of it is mystery, and you're the mystery. You're no professional dope dealer—you haven't the marks of it, you don't know enough about it, and you're the wrong temperament.

"You're a straight businessman—well, fairly straight. You've got a secret motive for this whole thing, and I want to follow through until I find out what it is."

I was impressed with his perspicacity, but I didn't show it. I left him in the dark. Let him enjoy the enigma—it would keep him motivated. I opened his door.

"Seven days," he said.

I went back to my hotel. After dinner I went to bed early. The next day I returned to England.

CHAPTER NINE

Richard Elliott was a fat man of thirty years with a split personality. He didn't know whether to be a staid, responsible, trustworthy type like accountants are supposed to be; or to be a trendy young professional, as befitted someone who had risen as far and as fast as he had.

In consequence he had short hair and huge sideburns; wore loud suits over white Marks and Spencer shirts with little collars; and talked an incongruous mixture of financial jargon and hip slang. He was a partner in a firm of accountants, but worked almost exclusively as an adviser to my companies.

I met him in the restaurant of an hotel in Park Lane. He had on a green suit with a red stripe, an old school tie, and widely flared trousers over ten-year-old Chelsea boots.

"I hear your daughter is ill," he said solicitously. "How is she?"

"It's nervous exhaustion," I lied. I had been to the hospital the previous day, when I arrived back in London. The doctor had told me there was a glimmer of hope: she had regained consciousness for a few minutes during the night. I told Elliott: "She is still critical."

"I'm sorry."

"I haven't seen her for years," I told him. "My wife got custody, and you know how it is . . . I had no idea."

"You look pretty rough yourself, man. You been worrying?"

"Yes. But I'm also tired. I've been over to France in the last few days, looking at the Paris deal." For some time I had been negotiating to buy a building plot in the suburbs of Paris. Now the transaction formed a vital part of my other plans—the ones I had to keep from Elliott. "Did you get my message to prepare the papers?"

"Yes."

"I want to hurry the deal. Another firm has been sniffing around, and if we don't get in quick the price may go up. How are we fixed?"

"The solicitors are in a position to proceed with the exchange of contracts. Now it's down to us to get the bread together."

"What have we got already?"

"We have £50,000 lying in the bank doing nothing but wanking," he said. I forgot to mention he was insufferably vulgar. "We have a promise of another hundred grand for the deal from the merchant bankers. That leaves us to raise £75,000."

We ordered steaks and a bottle of claret. I really prefer a rough wine with a bite, like Beaujolais, to wash down a steak. But these accountants like to stick with tried and tested combinations. I went along with Elliott. I had some pretty unorthodox suggestions to make later on.

I pondered the problem while he butchered his

lunch. By the time the brandy came I had figured how to put it to him.

He leaned back, brandy balloon in hand, and gave a contented sigh. Now was the time to hit him, I thought.

"What have I got that I can mortgage?" I asked.

He spluttered over a mouthful of very old cognac. "You're not playing bloody Monopoly, you know."

I decided to lean on him a little. "Just answer the question, lad."

He looked hurt, and said: "Nothing, then."

I played a high card. "Arseholes. What about the Oxford Street building?"

"Well, in theory we could raise fifty grand on it. But . . . "

"Theory, shmeory. In practice, working out the details is your problem. If we can raise fifty grand on it, we can raise fifty grand on it tomorrow."

"Tomorrow!" He sighed the sigh of those whose wearisome lot it is to explain the adult world to small children. "Apples, no one will lend you that kind of money at twenty-four hours notice."

"Make someone an offer they can't refuse."

"Stars, he's the Godfather now." How little he knew, how right he was.

It was my turn to sigh. "Must I do your job for you? Try Simon Davidson—they owe us a favour. Try . . . No, I've got it."

"Well?"

"Jones the Shop," I announced triumphantly, playing my ace.

"Who?"

"You know Jones Ltd, the department store chain."

"Has your brain got addled? They are shop-keepers. Why would they lend you money?"

"This is how you do it, Richard." The waiter gave him a cigar, and I lit it. First the iron glove, then the velvet fist. "Present the deal to Jones's as a rather risky venture. Make us look like a bunch of rather sharp operators. Give them the impression there's a good chance we'll welsh on the loan."

"What the hell good would that do?"

"Don't you see? They'd give their eye-teeth for that site in Oxford Street. It's mighty small, but it's a foot in the door. They'll lend us the money in the hope of foreclosing and getting the building."

He looked like somebody's maiden aunt who has been given a vibrator for Christmas. "You can't do business that way, Apples. Or at least, I can't. It in-volves making my firm look like a bloody suburban mortgage broker. I've got to think of the firm."

I laid a trump card. "All right, think of the firm. What proportion of its business comes from my out-fit?"

He looked uncomfortable. "About half, give or take."

"The way you're acting, you're giving—all of it—to another fucking company, man."

"I suppose I'll have to try it."

"And if it doesn't work, find another way. Now, that leaves £25,000 to raise." The final sum would be much more than I needed for the heroin. But I had to make it look like I was going ahead with the Paris purchase right up until the last moment; and for that deal I would have needed £25,000. "How much have I got in negotiable shares of my own?"

It was time for another splutter, and he did it right on cue. "Twenty, thirty grand. But . . . Listen, you had all this worked out beforehand, didn't you?"

"It's just as well, because you came up with sweet sod-all in the ideas department."

"Well this one won't work. For one, I can't let you lay your personal holdings on the line—there are much more sensible ways to raise money." He caught my eye, and went on hastily; "But anyway, if you unloaded the lot at once it would bring down the price of the bigger holdings."

"Only if you sell them all in the same place."

"Look, Apples, I'm an accountant, not a bloody magician."

"My account is on the line, Richard."

"Wow, you really know how to act the bastard. It must come naturally."

When he started to insult me I knew I had won. I concealed my relief. I laid a couple of tenners on the table and stood up. "No, finish your coffee," I said with a hand on his shoulder as he started to get up. "And the meal is on me."

"I should bloody well think so."

I leaned over and said in his ear: "Abracadabra."

He looked at me, mystified. "You're cracking up," he said. "What do you mean, abracadabra?"

"Practice saying it," I said, and went before he boiled over.

When I got home Annabel was lying on the floor, dressed in a bra. Although she had moderately massive tits, she never wore a bra under a shirt or dress. They stuck up quite nicely on their own. But she sometimes wore a bra and nothing else. I thought it looked quite nice.

She was reading a dirty book. I took it out of her hand and looked at it. It had glossy colour photos of a youth and a woman in a number of implausible positions.

I pointed to one of the pictures. "Anybody who knows anything about anatomy would tell you that position would snap it in half," I said.

"Perhaps he's got a jointed one," she said.

I dropped the book on the floor. "This sort of thing will lead you down the slippery slope of immorality."

She opened her legs and covered her pubes with her hand. "I've got a slippery slope," she said. "Come ski-ing with me."

I knelt between her knees and kissed everything within reach. There was a lot of it, and it took a while. Eventually I removed my face from her breast and said: "How's Babs?"

She sat up and started to undo my trousers. "She feels so well she's guilty about staying in bed. But I made her."

"Did you now. Let's go and make her again, you lustful old bag."

I stood up and walked toward the bedroom, leaving my trousers behind. With a whoop Annabel leapt on my back. I almost collapsed.

I staggered into the bedroom with one of Annabel's bullet-shaped boobs over each shoulder. Babs was lying asleep on the bed, the quilt thrown aside, and her scanty nightdress all awry. I stopped. I was still capable of being stunned by her beauty at odd moments. Annabel slid off my back.

She whispered: "Doesn't she look innocent?"

"Let's corrupt her," I murmured. Annabel went around to the other side of the bed. Gently, we lay down either side of Babs. Each of us took one small brown breast in our hands.

She stirred slightly without waking. Her black nipples grew hard under our light caresses. I slipped my hand over her belly and down between her thighs. Annabel's hand went inside my briefs, and it was like a small, frisky animal on my skin.

I kissed Babs' nose, and she opened her eyes. "Apples," she sighed. She kissed me, and then Annabel. It looked like I was forgiven. "It's nice to be the three of us again," Babs said.

Then things started getting complicated.

I slept the sleep of the fucked until late that evening. When I woke up I took a shower and went into the kitchen. Babs had several large slices of rare, cold roast beef and a salad ready for me.

It wasn't normal for the girls to cook for me. They weren't domestic labourers, and we worked as a triangle of equals. We usually cooked for ourselves or ate out, and the cleaning was done weekly by professionals.

"Bless you," I said to Babs. "But why salad at this time of year?"

"You're getting out of condition," she said with a

smile. "Too much carbohydrate."

"Out of condition?" I said. "Listen, not many men of my age could take two women to bed and—"

"All right, you did quite nicely. But afterwards you looked like a corpse. We thought you'd had a heart atack."

"Silly pair of old women. Only fat old men have heart attacks."

"Don't kid yourself."

"Ah well." I dug into the meal. Annabel got three cans of lager out of the fridge. I opened mine and took a long swallow. "You know, they sell this stuff in France. Same name, same label. But it tastes different." I drank some more.

My attempt at small talk fell flat on its back. I could see the pair of them were about to launch a pincer movement.

Annabel said: "Apples, will you tell us what the hell you've been doing for the last four days?"

In some ways the three of us were very close. But we had some unwritten rules, and one was that we never asked each other what we did when we were apart. We waited for information to be volunteered.

I told Annabel: "We don't usually ask each other that sort of question."

Her eyes blazed: "We don't usually go beating up junkies, chasing pushers, and getting beaten up and raped! And if you're putting your fool head on a block in some cowboy venture, you could at least put us in the picture."

I smiled grimly. The velvet fist, then the iron glove.

Babs put her hand on my wrist. "Apples, you might have been dead. We worried about you."

I pushed away my plate, feeling foolish and rather angry—not with them, but with myself. I had behaved like the kind of cowboy who says "This ain't wummin's business" and rides off into the night to get killed. Nothing makes me madder than being in the wrong.

I told them the whole thing. Then I felt better.

An hour later I parked the car near Charing Cross Station. I was wearing faded jeans and an old pair of boots. From the boot of the car I took a grubby raincoat and an old Donovan cap I kept there in case I ever had to change a wheel in the rain. I put them on.

As an afterthought, I rubbed my hands on a tyre and smeared some dirt on the backs of my hands and on my face. Then, doing my impression of a junkie, I shambled off in the general direction of Piccadilly Circus.

It was around midnight. There were people about, but they were thinning out. Anyone with any sense kept to the main streets, or took a cab. Only fools and hard nuts risked the back streets.

I like the West End at that time of night. The main streets are as bright as day with the lights from shop windows, and everyone is either enjoying themselves or up to no good. I like picking out the revellers, the lovers, the intending seducers, the country bumpkins, and the villains. Tonight I was interested in one particular type of villain.

I rounded Piccadilly Circus and walked up Shaftesbury Avenue. The last of the theatregoers had gone home, and the theatres were shutting up shop, but the amusement arcades were still alive with people spending their change. I went into one and hung around for a while, but didn't see what I was looking for. I bought a cup of revolting coffee from a machine.

I went out again and walked further north-east for 100 yards, then turned left. Now I was forsaking the relative safety of the bright lights for the gloom of Soho. A party of drunken miners spilled out of a strip club where no doubt they had been rooked, but they looked cheerful enough. They were singing the Welsh National Anthem. Occasionally a couple would step across the pavement from a restaurant to a waiting taxi. I passed a girl standing beside a lampost. She ignored me. A young man wearing a bow tie staggered up and asked me the way to the nearest Tube station. Playing my role, I told him to fuck off, and silently wished him luck in getting there without getting rolled.

I decided to change my tactics. I sat down in the doorway of a sandwich bar in which I would be visible but unobtrusive. I felt in my pocket for a cigarete. Before taking it out I bent it a little. Then I lit it with a match.

While I was waiting I had time to go over my plan, and I found it full of holes. I was hoping to get to Mr. H. by offering him a large consignment of heroin at a good price. I had bought so much that by the time I had made him the offer his supplies would be running out. I had to have that lever on him, to make him take the risk of buying from a source he didn't know.

But there were lots of other things he could do. He could still try to buy elsewhere—America, for example. He could simply shut up shop for a couple of weeks, and wait for the Marseilles refiners to catch up with demand.

And even if he did just what I wanted, that didn't guarantee me success. I would not show him my face until the very last minute, so why should he show me his? He could run the whole deal through underlings, and I might not even know.

I needed a second string to my bow, and I was tossing around in my mind for another approach when a fellow with long, straggly hair and a trench coat came briskly down the street. I forgot about strategy and turned my attention quickly to tactics. He looked like my mark.

I tossed the cigarette butt into the pavement to make sure he saw me. Sure enough, he took the bait.

He slowed his pace, looked at me, then came and leaned over me.

"Hey, man, want a fix?" he said.

I grabbed the broad lapel of his coat and pulled hard. He was taken by surprise, and fell to the ground beside me. I held him there.

"Hey, what is this?" he said in a frightened voice.

"Shut up and listen, punk," I told him. "Take this message to your governor. A new pipeline from Marseilles is open. Some very good stuff for £1,000 a kilo—but he has to buy a thousand kilos. Got it?"

"Where does he contact you?" he asked, not moving. Smart lad, this pusher.

"I contact him." I shoved him away. "Now move!" He got to his feet and padded off down the road.

I walked a short way in the opposite direction. That had gone off as planned, but there was still the problem of my second string. On impulse, I crossed the street and doubletracked back. I got within sight of the pusher as he was crossing Shaftesbury Avenue. I trailed him, but he didn't go far. Just to the Purple End.

CHAPTER TEN

First thing in the morning I went to County Hall to look up the entertainment licence for the Purple End. It was in the name of a Miss Wanda Dunhill, which meant nothing to me. Not that I cared. She almost certainly was a respectable front for the real owner. She probably was his mistress, too. I was more interested in the address she gave, which was a block of flats just off Sloane Square.

I left County Hall and got a cab on Westminster Bridge.

It was not so much a block of flats, as a large old

house which had had its insides gouged out and rebuilt. It was a very swank address. I hung around outside until the lobby was clear, then went in for a word with the janitor.

He had a flat in the basement. He came to the door in his braces.

"Have a drink with the *News of the World*," I said, and slipped a tenner to him. He folded it away in the breast pocket of his shirt.

"Come in," he said.

When he had sat me down in the lounge of his flat he said: "What can I do for you. sir?"

"Do you know this woman who lives in No. 11, Miss Dunhill?"

He stood up and took the tenner out of his pocket. "Sorry, sir, there's no one of that name living here." He proferred the tenner.

I held out two tenners. "Sure?"

"Positive." Christ, I thought, she must be bunging him considerably. I tried a oncer. He put it in his pocket and sat down again.

"Yes, since you're so persistent, there is a Miss Dunhill in eleven."

"She live on her own?"

"Most of the time."

I gave him a wink. "On the game?"

He frowned. "I suppose so, although she doesn't keep very busy."

"Any regular callers?"

"Yes, two. One of them's a toff. Comes in the afternoons. Every afternoon, for a couple of weeks, then you don't see him for a month. He's about at the moment. I expect he'll be there this afternoon."

"And the other?"

"You never know when he'll turn up. Ordinary-looking sort of bloke, but well loaded. A bit like yourself."

"Thanks." I laughed. "Any names?"

"No. No idea."

"Hmmm." I thought for a minute. "Is there any way I can get a look at them?" I slid another hundred across the table at him.

He looked worried then, and hesitated about picking up the note. But greed won out over fear. The note disappeared into that cavernous shirt pocket, and he said: "Well, as it happens, she has asked me to get someone to look at her central heating. I've got a plumber coming this afternoon. You'd have to pretend to be his mate. Then if the toff is there, you'll have a good chance of a look at him."

"You're on," I said. "What time?"

"Get here about three. You'd better wear overalls. I'll straighten it with the plumber—he's a mate."

I stood up. "Nice one, my friend." He saw me out.

I had to go to the bank before I could afford lunch—he had been a very expensive janitor. After lunch I went to Millett's and bought a pair of denim dungarees.

I arrived at the janitor's flat dead on three o'clock with my overalls in a paper bag under my arm. The plumber was waiting. I gave him a tenner and he asked no questions.

I carried his tool bag as we went up in the lift and

68

knocked on No. 11. The toff had been there for about fifteen minutes, so with luck he still would have his trousers on.

Miss Dunhill opened the door. She wore a silk pyjama suit, her hair was perfectly coiffeured, she smelt faintly of something expensive, and her make-up was superb. But she gave it all away when she opened her mouth.

"Oh, good, the heating engineer," she said.

Her refined accent had an undertone of Cockney in it, and besides, a real snotnose—like me—would have said "Ah, the plumber." She was a high-class tart.

She led us into the kitchen and showed us the boiler. The plumber took the front off and began to mess about inside. Miss Dunhill looked on, smoking. I had to admit she was a dish. The pyjama suit was semi-transparent, and under its loose folds she had a perfect old-fashioned figure-eight body: high, wide tits, a narrow waist, generous hips, and long legs.

I began to get restless, but it wasn't just the close proximity of Miss Dunhill. If we spent the whole time in the kitchen I never would get a look at the toff.

I said: "I better take a look at the rad in the lounge."

She said: "The first door on the left down the hall." Even the way she mouthed the words was erotic, and after she had spoken she wrapped her lips around the cigarette as if it were the prick of the year.

I opened all the other doors off the hall before I

got to the right one. There was a cupboard, a bathroom, and an empty bedroom. I went into the drawing room. That was empty too.

There was a long radiator under a big window in one wall. I fiddled with the tap for a minute, let some water leak on to the carpet, and tightened it again. This was getting desperate.

I found a cigarette in my overalls pocket and stuck it between my teeth. In the centre of the room was a small pocket lighter on an occasional table. I picked it up, lit my cancer tube with it, then looked at it.

It did not belong to Miss Dunhill, for it bore the initials J.St.C.R. These were vaguely familiar.

A door opened quietly and a man walked across the room to me. He had an unlit cigarette in his hand. He reached for the lighter and said: "May I?"

I gave him the lighter and said: "Sorry, I was just lighting a fag."

He grunted, pocketed the lighter, and turned away. But I had got a good look at him. And I knew the identity of our toff.

He was John St. Clair Robins, Junior Minister at the Foreign Office.

I left the place in a state of shock, after giving the janitor and the plumber another fifty each and making the plumber a present of my crisp new overalls. I tried to remember what I knew about Robins. Private Eye called him "fun-loving", which meant they knew he was a ram. But he was a fairly obscure Minister.

In the U.S.A. his thick blond hair and perfect teeth would have put him in line for the Presidency, but he was a fairly small fish in Westminster. He was aged about forty.

I needed to know a lot more about him. I took a taxi to the office of my old newspaper. Jack McIntyre, who had been a reporter with me, was now News Editor.

The place was much the same as I remembered it. They still hadn't replaced the clapped-out air conditioning, and the atmosphere was heavy with cigarette smoke. There were piles of copy paper, dozens of newspapers, and scattered wire trays all over the place. Everyone was on the phone, and half a dozen more were ringing plaintively. I stopped to look at the calendars, which were filthy. On the wall some joker had stuck the strapline from a rival paper's jobs page: "There's a better job for you in the *Daily Express*."

Jack was speaking into a telephone. "What we want now is an interview with the girl friend. When were they going to get married, was she worried about him, that sort of stuff. And if you can let us have something good by about nine we might get it on Page Three. O.K.? Bye."

He looked up. "Apples! It's nice to see you. What do you want, a job?"

"Hello, mate. How are you."

"Still struggling, my boy." He looked at his watch. "Buy you a drink?"

"No time, Jack. I came to ask two favours."

"Shoot."

"Can I use the library for a minute?"

71

"Sure. I hope the other favour's as easy as that."

"Will you ask your Political Editor where John St. Clair Robins will be tonight?"

"No problems. Go up to the library, and when you come back I'll have the answer."

The library gave me a file on Robins. He was a wine importer, and a fairly recent Cabinet appointment. Tory ladies liked his good looks and the P.M. liked his solid private-enterprise background. He had a good knowledge of Europe, particularly France, through his business; and he used it to deal with Common Market matters at the F.O. He had a safe Parliamentary seat and was tipped as a fast riser in the party. He was said to have a "good brain"—something so rare among politicians that profile writers always mention it.

When I got back to the news room Jack was talking to a dapper little man in a dark suit. "Apples, meet Arnold Crane, our Political Editor." We shook hands.

Crane said: "Robins is going to a reception at the Dutch Embassy tonight at nine. After that he's got nothing official."

"Thanks," I said. "Are you going?"

"I've got an invite, but I won't be there," he replied. "It's only a bullshit do, to welcome some minor new diplomat. Ritual rubbish."

"I don't suppose you'd let me use your invitation."

Crane looked at Jack, who nodded slightly. "Sure," said Crane. He reached into his pocket and pulled out a white card with black copperplate script on it.

I said: "I'm grateful to you. If I come across anything, I'll let you know it."

Crane said: "Why, have you got the smell of something?"

"Maybe. But you tell me: how does Robins smell to you?"

Crane thought for a moment. "Bad," he said.

"That is interesting. Why?"

"He should have it all going for him. He's well-liked, and able. If he wanted it he could be the next P.M., or the next but one." He thought for a minute. "But he seems to hold himself back. Take this Common Market job. He could have done better than that in the last reshuffle. He could have held out for a lesser Ministry. And nobody quite knows why. He may have a dark secret."

"I have a feeling you're right," I said. "I can't say too much, but look out for a major scandal involving Robins within a month."

I stood up. Jack said: "Let us know first, won't you."

"Sure thing," I said, nodded to Crane, and left. As I crossed the office floor Jack called: "And next time, give yourself time for a few beers."

I called home from a kiosk outside, and spoke to Annabel. "Want to meet some top people tonight?" I said.

"No bloody thanks," she replied.

"For me," I persisted. "I need an escort."

She sighed. "Do you want me to hold your prick while you pee?"

"Hmm, kinky. We'll talk about it later. Meanwhile, try to find a respectable dress. You know,

73

one that covers your pubes and your tits both. See you soon."

When I got home I put on my penguin suit. Annabel found a long dress through which you only just could see her nipples. We kissed Babs goodbye.

"Don't worry about me. I wouldn't come if I were asked. I simply must watch this marvellous BBC2 documentary on superstition in Ancient Egypt," she said sarcastically.

"I'm afraid the diplomatic world is one in which our little threesome might not be understood for the innocent, platonic relationship it really is," I said. She laughed.

"I don't really mind, you mug."

As we left she shouted: "Bring me back a nice big black man. A young one."

We took a taxi, as I might get pissed and Annabel certainly would. On the way I told her I was interested in Robins.

"The system has to work like this," I said. "The French side get the stuff to Robins whenever he is in Europe—Paris, Brussels, Luxembourg, he visits them all frequently. He uses his status to get the stuff into this country, probably in fairly small quantities—but a suitcaseful every week is a lot of heroin. He takes it to the Sloane Square flat and leaves it with Miss Dunhill. She passes it on to her other visitor, who is probably Mr. H. From there it goes to the Purple End and doubtless half a dozen other major outlets."

At the Embassy we handed over our invitation and asked the doorman not to announce us. We managed to slip in without being introduced to the minor dignitary for whom the bash was being put on.

"You've built up this picture on pretty slender evidence," Annabel murmured as we circulated, smiling politely at complete strangers.

"Yes, but I've got a feeling about Robins."

"Oh, yes?"

"Yes, and I'd like you to feel him too. There he is." I pointed him out.

"Oh, I know him," she said. "Johnny Robins. He thinks he's incredibly sexy."

"And is he?"

"I don't know."

"How would you like to find out?"

She looked at me speculatively. Then she looked at Robins again. "Well, he looks fit."

"Attagirl. We'll work our way around to him."

Annabel knew some of the people there, although she liked none of them. But we had to make polite conversation with several as we worked our way through the crowd. When we got there Robins was flashing his teeth at some dowager. Annabel introduced me.

I had a tense moment when I wondered whether he would recognise me from that afternoon. But he only had looked at me briefly, and he was the kind who really never sees the faces of workmen. And if I did look vaguely familiar, he would assume I was one of the many forgettable faces he had been introduced to at countless parties like this one.

He smiled and introduced me to his Press Secretary, who was a cracking little bit of stuff. Press Secretary my foot, I thought. He immediately turned his teeth on Annabel, who wiggled her bosom appreciatively. I left her to deal with him, and looked at the secretary.

She was very small, with short blonde hair and a perfect tan. Her name, most inappropriately, was Gertrude.

"Do they call you Dirty Gertie?" I asked her.

She looked me up and down and decided she liked. "Some of them," she said.

I told her I had been a reporter and she changed the subject a bit sharp. She clearly didn't want me to find out the extent of her knowledge of Press matters.

"Do you know Alastair John, the designer?" she asked conversationally.

I know Alastair John the pusher, I thought. Still, everyone had to have a front. "Yes," I said. If Robins knew him too, that would prove he kept bad company.

"He's having a party tonight. We're going on there after this dull old do is over," she went on. "Are you?"

"Well, well," I said. We are now, anyway, I thought. Gertrude couldn't have been to one of Al's parties before, or she wouldn't be so quick to tell strangers she was going there.

But it put Robins very clearly in perspective. I doubted whether he had a direct tie-up with Alastair; but no respectable politician would be a friend of Al's.

I was well pleased. Robins was the second string to my bow.

I turned to Annabel. Robins was lighting her

cigarette with the lighter I had seen that afternoon. He looked at me. I had another nasty moment, but it passed.

"We may be seeing Mr. Robins later," I told Annabel.

Robins beamed. I was getting sick of his teeth. I wondered whether I might get the chance to knock some of them out. Stupid bugger, I told myself, he'd slaughter you.

He said: "Oh, really? How delightful. At Alastair's?"

"Yes." We nodded politely and eased away.

We found the buffet, but it was lousy. Whoever puts on these receptions is always so unimaginative—you get the same old vol-au-vents, smoked salmon sandwiches, and little bits of salty nothing on biscuits every time.

"Let's see if Al can do better," I said.

"I thought the moment would never come," Annabel replied.

It was still fairly early when we got to Alastair's. It was someone's birthday, and the guests were having a whale of a time playing pass-the-parcel, oranges-and-lemons, and hunt-the-thimble. It was a typical wacky Alastair party.

I sat down and watched the fun, contemplating my lost childhood and waiting for the party to really warm up. As I expected, the games started to get rather dirty, with clothes being shed here and there.

The contrast between the two parties I went to that night hardly could have been more striking: the Embassy, with its chandeliers and bow ties and the clink of empty conversation; and less than a mile away at Al's, the roar of laughter and the blurring of sexual roles. As if to emphasise the contrast, a girl started doing a strip in the middle of the floor. A small group gathered around her. She was small and rather muscular, and it was not until she took off her bra that we realized she was a bloke.

Robins came in with Gertrude then, and I reflected that he was trying to belong to two worlds: the world of the embassies and the world of the Alastairs. I doubted whether it could be done—before long one of the worlds would reject him.

In the corner a young man with spectacles was looking at Al's bookshelf, in the way people do when they get bored at parties. Annabel was off somewhere playing coalman's knock, and I struck up a conversation with the bespectacled youngster to avoid getting involved in the games. He was looking at Wittgenstein's Philosophical Investigations, and I started to explain the book to him as I covertly watched Robins.

Al had laid on a purple light for this bash. By this time he had dimmed it so that everyone now looked like a bruised corpse. There was a different record playing in every room in the house, and with all the doors open it sounded like an orchestra tuning up in a traffic jam.

The light turned Robins' blond hair a kind of orange, and darkened his suntan to black, and when the purple light flashed on his teeth he looked like something out of a horror film. He stayed on the fringes of the party, smiling occasionally at the antics of the other guests and drinking quite hard. I watched the way he lit cigarettes, sipped his drink, stroked his chin and put his hands in and out of his pockets. I noticed the little nervous habit he had of fiddling with his jacket buttons, undoing them and doing them up again. He kept scanning faces in the room, and once or twice I caught him looking at the door.

Then Annabel found him and I turned the surveillance over to her. Despite his outward suavity, I had decided he was a worried man.

She knew what I wanted to know most, and she was going to remember any names Robins mentioned. It was all we could do.

The two of them disappeared, and I continued my conversation with the bookworm, who turned out to be a student. Our conversation was getting drunker and drunker. About the time we stopped making sense, Gertrude crawled over. I was lying on my back, drinking through a child's bendy straw from a glass beside my head. Gertrude sort of slithered on top of me.

Removing the straw from my mouth, she put her lips to my ear and said: "My man has gone off with your woman." She pronounced it "gorn orff" in a superb imitation of Robins' accent, and I laughed.

I put both hands behind her and worked her long dress up until it was above her waist. I looked down over her shoulder and saw that she had neat, hard buttocks and fine slender legs. I put one hand under the elastic of her knickers and worked it around the cleft of her rump until her fanny nestled comfortably in my palm.

"Where have they gone?" I said.

"Upstairs," she mumbled into my shoulder.

"Shall we go and watch them at it?" I said in her ear.

She lifted her head and looked at me. An erotic gleam came into her glazed eyes. She wet her lips with her tongue, nodded, and breathed: "Yes, let's."

I held on to her knickers as she stood up, pulling them down over her knees to her feet. The long dress fell around her ankles and she stepped out of the panties. Nothing turns me on like a bird in a long dress and no knickers.

The student was saying: ". . . makes it plain that the search for a primary unit of perception—such as a sense-datum—is a wild goose chase."

I stood up. "Ah, but what about the duck-rabbit?" I said, and left him.

We pushed our way through the crowd. The ground floor of the house was packed now, and the air was heavy with the smell of joss-sticks, sweet and slightly decaying.

The people were the usual multi-sexual mixture, and with the darkness and their unisex clothes you needed to see them naked before you knew whether they were male or female. As it happened many of them were naked or half-naked, and I got a hard-on just pushing my way through the crush. On the way I recognized a new pop star, two famous film directors and a member of the House of Lords.

Upstairs was quieter. We poked our heads into a big room. There was no furniture. A dozen people were sitting in a circle on a vast carpet around a complicated arrangement of flasks and tubes which reminded me of fourth-form chemistry experiments. Robins was in the circle, his jacket and tie discarded and his hair disarrayed. He was sitting between Annabel's spread legs with a rubber tube in his mouth. He took a deep draw, blew out smoke, and passed the tube to the next person in the circle.

Gertrude looked at me wide-eyed. "Oh!" she said. "The Minister is smoking pot!"

I laughed. I stood behind Gertrude and put my hands on her breasts. She took a step backward and pressed against me, moving her bottom from side to side against my thighs.

We stood in the doorway and watched the people in the room getting high. There was soft conversation and a lot of giggling. One man had become engrossed in the pattern of the carpet, measuring the blocks of colour with his shoes and mumbling mathematical formulae. A girl had taken off her shirt and was quietly massaging her own nipples. Another girl was making funny faces, and the people next to her would occasionally shriek with laughter, obliterating the classical guitar music playing on the stero.

. I saw Robins roll over and face Annabel. He slowly unbuttoned the front of her dress, then put his hand inside on her breast. As if that were a signal, the pot party began to degenerate into an orgy. People took off their clothes with gay abandon. The carpet analyst traced a streak of red all the way to the girl with no shirt, and started analysing her instead.

I felt Gertrude's nipples harden under my

fingers. About time, too, I thought.

I took my hands from her breasts and lifted the back of her dress. She put her hands behind her back and unzipped the fly of my formal trousers. As the orgy got under way, I slipped inside her from behind. I took hold of her hips and moved her back and forward.

Her eyes stayed fixed on Robins, who was rutting away enthusiastically now, blind—like everyone in the room—to the people all around him. I moved one hand under her dress around her hip to her pubis, and pressed with the heel of my palm. She began to breathe hard. I was quite enjoying myself, too.

Robins gave a shout which I recognised as being terminal. Gertrude yelled: "Oh, Johnny!" and came at the same time as Robins.

I was not very flattered.

"What did you find out?" I asked Annabel in the taxi on the way home.

"Two things," she said. "One: he has false teeth."

"Really? If that got out it could ruin his political career. What's the other thing?"

"A man gave him a thick envelope which he furtively stuffed in his pocket. It could have contained a lot of ten-pound notes."

I looked at the street lights flashing by through the window of the cab. "The pay-off," I mused. "Who was the man?"

"Nobody I recognised."

"Nobody important, either, I expect. Ah well, at least we both got laid. What was Robins like in the sack?"

"Competent but uninspired."

"Like his politics."

"What was his secretary like?"

"She was inspired all right—by Robins. She didn't take her eyes off him while I was screwing her."

"Perhaps she was looking at me."

"Is there no end to your egotism?" I kissed her.

It was five a.m. when we rolled into the flat. Marjory, my ex-wife, was sitting on the couch with Babs in the grey dawn light. Both of them had been crying.

In my drunken state I found the situation competely baffling. "Marjory?" I said. "Here?"

She said: "Apples, Jane has had a relapse. They say there's no hope."

CHAPTER ELEVEN

I woke up at noon with an end-of-the-world grade hangover. The pain started just behind my eyes and went along under my skull to the back of my neck. And my guts felt distinctly seasick. I put on a robe and went looking for medication.

I was very tempted by the vodka bottle, but exercised my will-power and yielded not. I was going to have a hangover and there was no point postponing it. I found two grapefruit in the fridge and ate them both. They improved the taste of my mouth, so I lit a cigarette to make it taste foul again. Then I rang Richard Elliott.

I asked him: "How are we doing?"

He said: "Uh, it's cool, man."

"Talk English, you overgrown hippie. Have you raised the money or not?"

"By tomorrow morning your Paris bank account will be in credit in the sum of £225,000. In other words I scored, baby, and now I'm going home."

"At midday?"

"Do you think I've had time to raise your stinking money and sleep as well?"

"Pleasant dreams, Richard."

"Love and peace, arsehole." He hung up. I sat back and drew on my cigarette. I felt 'relieved: I hadn't been at all sure that we would get the money in time. Another hurdle had been crossed. But I had another lead to follow up.

I dialled the Yard and asked for Arthur Lambourne.

"Hello, Apples," he said. "What have you got for me?"

"Nothing you haven't got already, if you're any good as a copper."

"Try me."

"What do you know about the Purple End?"

"Refined people like you aren't often seen there. It's frequented by low criminal types like Harry Hat. One of 100 middle-level nightclubs in the West

End. It's almost certainly victim of a protection racket, but it will have skeletons of its own in the cupboard.

"Who runs it?"

"I don't know off-hand. You could look up the licence."

"No, I mean who really runs it."

"Sorry, Apples. Is it important?"

"Yes. Can you find out?"

"I expect so. Ring me tomorrow."

"No can do," I said. "I'm catching the six o'clock ferry from Dover. I'll get in touch when I get back."

"I'll do my best," he said. "Listen, Apples —should we be interested in the Purple End?"

"I think it might repay investigation."

"So what game are you playing?"

I hesitated, then said: "I'm looking for a syringe in a haystack." Then I hung up.

My hangover was still with me, so I decided to take time out to nurse it.

I took a hot shower and rubbed myself dry with a big, soft towel. Then I shaved with a safety razor, taking my time, using scented pre-shave and after-shave. I covered myself with talc.

I put on a clean lilac shirt, crisp black cotton trousers, and a soft grey jacket. I combed my hair and laced my shoes.

I poured a cup of black coffee, sat in an easy chair in front of the living room window, and lit a cigarette.

The Thames never fails to soothe me. It's grey, slow river with dirty grey buildings on either side, and even in bright sunlight it never seems to sparkle like rivers are supposed to. It is a good river for suicides, speaking of oblivion in the low sweep of its murky depths. None of the boats move very fast, even the river police's power boats, and there is so little traffic that you often see nothing at all for minutes on end. Then very occasionally a great beautiful boat will glide gracefully upstream, looking like a butterfly in a nettle patch. The speed of the river hardly alters in hundreds of years, unmoved by the increasingly frenetic pace of life all around it.

When I finished my coffee my hangover was receding. I packed a case quickly, whispered goodbye to a still-sleeping Annabel, and went down to the car.

By the time I rolled off the ferry into France, the day had turned into a beautiful evening. The air tasted warm and clean, and the sky cast a clear light although the sun was sinking. I had plenty of time. I planned to spend the night in Paris, take all tomorrow to drive down to Marseilles, and go to the Le-Grand villa the day after tomorrow—the seventh day.

As I pulled out of the ferry terminal on to the road, a girl stepped on to the kerb and lifted her thumb. It was my lucky day.

I stopped and wound the window down. "A Paris?" I asked.

"Oui, merci bien," she replied. She walked around the front of the car and got into the passenger seat beside me. She carried a small duffle bag

86

which she tossed into the back seat. I pulled away again.

"Anglais?" she asked me.

"Oui. Et vous?"

"Moi aussi." We both burst out laughing.

"What's taking you to Paris?" I asked her.

"Actually, I'm going to the South," she said. "I have relatives there who offered me a free holiday, and being a poor student I'm taking them up on it. All I have to do is get there—which is what I'm trying to do now. What about you?"

"I'm on my way to Marseilles. Business trip." I looked at her speculatively. She looked too old to be a student. She was a tall girl—almost as tall as me—with an old-fashioned figure: large breasts, and hips which were wider than was trendy at the time. She wore blue corduroy trousers, a check shirt and a long denim jacket. She had big, wide eyes and a rather Roman nose. She never would have made a career modelling, but she was quite bewitching.

She looked at me and looked away, embarrassed. She knew what I was thinking—that she could have a lift all the way to Marseilles with me, but it would mean an overnight stop. I decided to leave the idea unspoken for a while.

"What kind of music do you like?" I asked her.

She smiled. "Oh, old stuff. Mid-sixties—Beatles, Stones, you know. Stuff from my teenybopper days."

I sorted through my tapes and put on the Who's rock opera, *Tommy*. She settled comfortably in her seat and looked at the scenery. "This is nice," she said.

I didn't ask her what "this" was. I felt it myself—the peaceful French evening, the music, the soft hum of the car as it effortlessly ate up the miles. I passed her a packet of cigarettes.

"Thanks," she said. She lit two from the dashboard lighter and put one in my mouth. We didn't speak for a while. The evening dimmed into night, and I switched on the powerful quartz-halogen headlights. They cut a wedge of white in the darkness. The opera ended with We're Not Gonna Take It, and I switched the tape deck off.

"Hungry?" I said.

"I'm O.K. I've got some sandwiches in my bag."

"Feed them to the ducks and let me buy you dinner."

"It's kind, but you don't have to."

"I know I don't have to, but I'd like to."

"All right. Thank you."

We were a few miles out of Paris when I pulled off the road and followed a country lane for a couple of hundred yards. It was darker than ever away from the highway, and we almost passed the restaurant. I had never been there before, but it was in the Michelin guide.

It was an old farmhouse, with the restaurant itself in what had once been a barn. The rest of the building was given over to bedrooms.

A waiter showed us to a table. There were polished floorboards and a dim, flickering light from oil-lamps on the walls. The waiters were all old, which pleased me—I hate cocky young waiters who try to give the impression waiting is rather beneath them.

The meal was magnificent, and we both ate with relish. We took a long time over it, and we finished three bottles of wine before we got to the cheese. We were drinking a delicious pear liqueur and waiting for the coffee to cool when the girl leaned over the table to me. Her face was slightly flushed. Her shirt had mysteriously become undone at the top and I looked fondly at the smooth curve of a breast.

She said: "Why don't we stay the night here—then I could come all the way to Marseilles with you tomorrow."

I was too pissed to be polite. "You're on," I told her. "Shall we have it off tonight?"

"And I thought you were refined," she said.

"Even refined people like to have a bit of nooky," I said. "How about it?"

"Well, I don't usually, but I will for you, you sweet-talking bugger."

The sun woke me early in the morning. I had to think for a minute before I remembered who belonged to the dark hair on the pillow beside me.

I got up, feeling fit and full of energy, and went to the window. The sunshine was steaming the dew off the flat French fields, and when the haze cleared it would be hot.

When I got out of the bath the girl was slipping into her bra. "Good morning," I said, and kissed her.

"How can you be so cheerful so early," she said, pulling on her trousers.

"Clean living," I said solemnly.

We had coffee and croissants, then I paid the bill and we drove into Paris. I hired a white Citroen there, and garaged the Jaguar. The girl asked no questions, and I offered her no explanations. We bought some food and a picnic basket, and drove on in the new car.

It was a perfect blue-sky day, and as we sped down the autoroute with the windows open, the fresh air blew my troubles out of my mind for a few hours. I enjoyed the girl's company—she was young and innocent and continually bubbling over with laughter. We stopped by the roadside to eat our picnic, then we made love again in the open air with the traffic roaring by a few yards away.

It was evening again when we got to Marseilles. I pulled off the road near a roundabout on the main road. The girl shouldered her duffle bag, opened the door, and kissed me.

"Thank you for a lovely interlude," I said.

"Thank you for the ride," she said with a grin. She got out of the car. Then she turned back to me.

"What's your name?" she said.

"If I told you, you wouldn't believe me."

She grinned again and closed the door. I pulled away, leaving her at the kerb with a faraway smile on her face.

CHAPTER TWELVE

In the morning I put on my bottle-green suit and my responsible businessman's face and took a taxi to the Pension Blanc. I half expected to be told Guy had decamped, but it turned out that my first-time assessment of him had been correct. However, he looked completely different.

His beard and moustache were gone, and his hair was cut shorter than mine. His jeans and grubby T-shirt had been replaced by dark trousers with a crease and a smart sports jacket.

He pointed to a small green Fiat in the parking lot next to the pension. "That's the car I hired in Paris," he said.

We got in and he drove out of town toward the LeGrand villa. I asked him: "Why the metamorphosis?"

"If you're going to be a drug smuggler you can't afford to look like a junkie," he said simply. He was dead right. The only thing he didn't know was that he wouldn't be smuggling any drugs.

I asked: "Everything else go off all right?"

"Yup. I bought a four-ton Scania and a load of fire-damaged soap powder. Dishwasher stuff, it is, packed in small drums. White as the driven snow, and very fine. The soap is in the lorry and the lorry is in a garage I've rented on the riverside in Paris."

"Export papers?" He tapped his pocket.

So far, so good, I thought. Now for the tough bit.

We parked in front of the villa and the butler with the misshapen face opened the door. He gave me a dirty look. When his face was expressionless it made me want to turn and run, but when he scowled it was enough to turn milk into yoghurt. But he showed us into the library without slipping a stiletto into my back.

LeGrand was expecting us, and his lawyer was with him. The lines of a song came unbidden into my head: "Bring your lawyer and I'll bring mine, Get together and we could have a bad time," and I wondered briefly where they came from.

We shook hands all around and LeGrand poured drinks. Guy said No, but I was feeling nervous and accepted a large Scotch.

Finally the lawyer said: "We have worked out a financial scheme which I hope will meet with your favour, Mr. Large." He opened a briefcase by his feet and drew out some papers.

"Shoot," I said.

"I beg your pardon?"

"I mean, go ahead and explain."

"Ah, yes. We—that is, M. LeGrand's organisation—own a trucking firm. It is a legitimate company, with a number of perfectly normal contracts, and it is run most efficiently. But its main value to us is for moving around the country all sorts of goods which we distribute unofficially, which—ah, shall we say, the police would be interested in."

I could guess what he meant. Drugs, stolen property, arms, forged notes—if LeGrand owned a fleet of lorries his organisation was probably into every major racket.

The lawyer went on: "Because of this, the firm actually makes no profit. When they are running our special trips, the lorries are officially idle and the drivers laid off. Any loss the firm makes we disguise in one way or another, thus contriving to break even. When necessary, the firm is used as a tax loss.

"Our plan is that you will buy this firm from us for just over a million francs—in fact, for the exact equivalent of £100,000. You will then lease the company back to us. We will not pay you a fixed rent, but we will agree to pay you a certain percentage of the profits, which of course will be nil."

It was a good plan. It would look as if I were injecting an ailing firm with a dose of capital in the hope of making it profitable. Eventually I would be seen to have made a poor investment—but that was not a crime.

He handed me a file. "Perhaps you will look over the paperwork. Meanwhile, we will clear your cheque with the bank—I take it you have the money in a French bank?"

"Yes." I wrote out a cheque and handed it to him.

"Excuse me, then," he said, and went out.

I looked at the contracts. My French is fluent, even if my accent is terrible, but I'm not up to legal jargon. However it hardly mattered. If they tried to pull a fast one they would have to take it to court to get it enforced, and the last thing LeGrand would want was any of his deals dragged through courts. Similarly, if I tried to double-cross them they would simply take out a contract on my life with a professional extermination organisation like the Mafia. The contract was a formality—a farce, simply there for show. Nevertheless I read it.

I made out a clause giving the board of directors power to veto any re-sale of the company before or after my death. That made sense—and it meant that all they had to do eventually was to let the business get into heavy debt then buy it back from me for a song. It was an intelligent arrangement. I didn't think LeGrand had conceived it. Either he had very clever people working for him, or he was working for someone else. But there was no point speculating about that—I had enough trouble trying to find the English Mr. H.

The lawyer came back and pronounced himself satisfied with my cheque, and I signed the papers. Now I was committed. There was no turning back.

LeGrand led us across to the other side of the house. He opened a door in a wall, revealing a flight of stone steps leading down. We followed him down the steps and found ourselves in a cellar. He threw a switch and bathed the place in harsh fluorescent light. Then he pointed to a corner.

There was an innocent-looking pile of red polythene sacks worth a million pounds on the London market.

I was carrying a small black suitcase. Before I left London I had spent some time in the pharmacology section of a medical school library.

In the case I had a child's chemistry set and one

or two extras. I put the case on a table and opened it. It took me ten minutes to set up the equipment. Then I took one of the red sacks at random from near the bottom of the pile and opened it.

I put a pinch of the white powder on a spatula and tipped it into a flask. A few seconds later I turned to LeGrand. "It's good," I said.

Guy put a few grains on his thumbnail, put his thumb to his nose, and sniffed hard. He threw his head back and closed his eyes for a moment. Then he nodded.

"Grade-A," he said.

LeGrand carefully resealed the sack I had opened. "Well, gentlemen, shall we supervise the loading?"

We went back up the steps and out to the back of the villa. Our Fiat already had been driven around from the front. LeGrand opened a trapdoor in the ground which led to the cellar we had just left.

Half a dozen assorted villains, including my friend the butler, appeared and went to work. One got down in the cellar and threw up the sacks to another, who caught them and stacked them neatly. The other four started taking the car apart.

The carpets came up, the doors came off, the seats were unbolted, the dashboard unscrewed, and finally the car was jacked up and the wheels removed.

The springs and the stuffing came out of the back seat and were replaced by heroin. More of the sacks went into the door panels, a few were put in the sills, and one behind the dash. A couple were taped inside each wing above the wheels and secured there with a welded metal plate. The whole thing took about an hour.

When the car was put back together again it looked as good as new. They had obviously done this sort of thing before.

I was glad to say good-bye to LeGrand, his villains and his lawyer. "I hope we will be able to do business again," I lied as I shook his hand. Then Guy and I got in the car and drove off.

We went to my hotel where I checked out. Then I showed Guy the Citroen. "All part of covering my tracks," I explained. "You take this car and stick close behind me. If there's any trouble, I want you around."

He grinned. "If you have an accident, don't expect me to stop."

We filled up with petrol in the town then set out for Paris. It was a hell of a drive.

I was behind the wheel of the most valuable car ever driven. It only needed some idiot to get careless and dent my door——and French drivers are among the worst in the world——and the snowy powder would spill all over the road, screaming my guilt to the world.

I kept rigidly to 10 m.p.h. below the speed limit. When it started to get dark I was the first to put my lights on. It began to rain steadily, and I had to peer hard into the distance. I was chain-smoking.

I opened the window to clear the air in the car when I felt a headache coming on. The rain blew in, soaking my shirt sleeve, and the wind was cold, but it served to keep me alert. I silently cursed every driver who came a little too near.

We were about 80 miles from Paris when the car started to behave peculiarly. The back tended to slip on the slightest bend. I almost wept. I slowed right down and nursed the wheel, but it got worse.

Guy was right on my tail by now in the Citroen. I gave in: pulled over, braked, and stopped in a lay-by. The rain was pelting down. The Citroen stopped behind the Fiat and Guy and I got out of the cars.

"What's the matter?" he yelled, trying to make himself heard above the noise of the wind, the rain and the traffic.

"The fucking car—swaying about all over the fucking road!"

If we had mechanical trouble we were just about doomed. As soon as they started to take the car apart they would find the stuff.

We walked all around the Fiat looking at the wheels in the light of the Citroen's headlamps. All the tyres were hard. I cursed.

"It must be the suspension," I yelled at Guy.

"Hold on," he shouted back. He was kneeling down beside the offside rear wheel. I knelt beside him on the wet tarmac.

The plate LeGrand's boys had welded under the wing had come loose and was dragging on the tyre. "We'll have to get it right off," I told Guy.

I took hold of the plate and heaved. It was as firm as a rock.

Guy said: "Pliers."

There was a pair in the boot of the Citroen and another in the Fiat. We each took one pair, clamped them on to the plate, and heaved. It didn't budge.

By this time we were both soaked to the skin and shivering. The rain was pouring down my face and I could hardly see. The plate was also wet, and slippery with mud and grease thrown up from the road, making it difficult to grip.

"Once more," I said.

We took hold, squeezed with all our might, and pulled.

It came away. We both fell over backwards into the wet road, drenched but jubilant.

Guy eased the plate out under the wheel arch, and the red plastic sacks slid neatly into my arms.

There was a screech of tyres and a car pulled up behind the Citroen. Two motorcycles pulled off the road in front of the Fiat. As I stood in the lay-by with two sacks of heroin cradled in my arms, I saw gendarmes jump out of the car and off the bikes. Four of them.

CHAPTER THIRTEEN

My mind went blank. I stood stock still as the policemen walked around the Citroen toward me. Behind me, I heard the powerful motorcycle engines die and the thud of boots on the tarmac.

For what seemed ages—although it only could

have been a few seconds—my brain was in neutral: the engine revving like mad but no power being transmitted to the wheels. All I could think about was how badly I would miss my freedom when I was rotting in a stinking, airless French jail. I thought of Bab's soft, rounded body, and the gleam of perspiration on Annabel's throat in the heat of love. I remembered the taste of rare steak and the bite of a good dry claret; the sound of Eric Clapton's guitar on the wings of inspiration, and the colour of the head on a pint of draught Guinness. I was paralysed by blind terror.

I hardly felt Guy snatch the bright red sacks out of my arms. I vaguely saw him open the boot of the Fiat, throw in the sacks and the metal plate, and slam the lid. I heard him in French shouting imprecations about the weather to the gendarmes, saw him raise his hands to the sky in a typically French gesture, then point at the wheel then at me. I caught the words "Anglais . . . fou . . . le pneu . . ."

One of the policemen began to speak rapidly, jabbing a finger in the air. I followed the direction he was pointing in and saw a sign forbidding stopping. It began to dawn on me that we hadn't been rumbled after all: still, the very presence of the law meant we might be any minute.

Guy took out his international driving licence and handed it over. A gendarme opened it and a note fell out into his hand. Guy looked the other way while he pocketed it and handed the licence back.

Then, as if all he wanted in the world was to get in out of the rain, Guy shouted. "Au revoir!" and got into the Citroen. I did the same with the Fiat. As I pulled into the road, I saw in my mirror the policemen returning to their vehicles.

In the car the warmth, the lights, and the steady rush of wind and rain gradually nursed me back to reality. I felt the cosy reassurance of the interior of the car, and the comforting monotony of the miles flying by under the wheels. The whole episode took on the unreal character of a dream.

As I changed into top gear I snapped out of the daze and let out a sigh: "Jesus wept, what a break," I sighed.

Guy overtook me as we approached Paris. I followed the tail lights of the Citroen through the city toward the river, then around a series of side-streets and dock roads. We finally pulled up on a cobbled forecourt in front of a big garage.

The building, like a small aeroplane hanger, stood on its own in a poorly-lit industrial area. The sound of the Seine lapping its banks was louder than the distant roar of the city's night-time traffic, and our feet on the cobblestones sounded like thunder. Guy keyed the lock and I pulled back the sliding door with a squeal of grazed metal.

I drove the Fiat straight in and Guy reversed the Citroen in after it. By the time he killed the motor I was sliding the door shut.

In the darkness he found a light switch. The half-dozen lamps hanging from the high ceiling were bright, but their illumination was mostly lost in vastness of the garage. In the yellow light I saw the lorry.

Guy had bought well: she was a powerful-looking box van with shiny paintwork, a year or so old but in apparently good nick. However I had no time for a thorough inspection—a nosey policeman might see the light in the old garage and come to investigate, and I wanted to get out of there as soon as possible.

I pulled down the tailgate. The box was packed with small cardboard drums about two feet high. Most of them were sooty and scorched; a lot were actually charred, and one or two were falling to pieces. I started to unload the better ones. Working as fast as I could after the long drive, I wheeled them to the edge of the box then stacked them on the ground.

The bad ones I moved around so as to leave a clear path down the centre of the wagon and a little circle of emptiness at the front end.

Meanwhile Guy was taking the Fiat to bits, and by now he had two piles beside the car: one of components and one of red sacks.

I opened one of the cardboard drums I had unloaded. Inside was a transparent polythene bag of white powder, gathered at the top and fastened with a piece of wire embedded in a strip of paper. I lifted the bag out of the drum and dragged it across the concrete to a filthy, stained sink in the corner by the door. I turned the tap experimentally. It worked.

I undid the bag and tipped the powder into the sink, then turned on the tap faster to wash away the detergent.

I took the empty back back over to the lorry. Suddenly Guy hissed: "Quiet!"

He padded swiftly over to the light switch and turned it out. Then I heard the voices of two men. I dived under the lorry, to find Guy already there.

We held our breath and listened.

"Qu'est-ce?" came a voice.

"Rien," said another. The voices sounded disinterested and bored. Then:

"Attention."

The other man gave an inquiring grunt.

"Ecoutez."

"D'eau . . ."

I cursed silently. I had left the tap running.

The door rattled. Then the first voice—the troublemaker, I had labelled him—said in a surprised tone: "Ouverte."

The second man gave another bored grunt.

The door slid open. From under the lorry I could see, silhouetted against the lighter dark of the outside, two pairs of legs partly covered by capes. The rain recently had stopped, and a little water dripped from the capes on to the oily concrete floor.

A torch flashed briefly over the semi-dismantled Fiat and homed on the sink.

"Regardez."

Grunt.

The troublemaker walked over to the tap and turned it off. Then he walked back and leaned on the door. There was silence for a few seconds.

"Cigarette?"

"Ah, merci."

A match flared and died, and a few more long seconds passed.

"Eh bien. Allons."

The door shut again and their footsteps receded

into the night. I breathed a prayer of thanks for the incompetence of French policemen. The dullest English bobby would have shone his torch around the garage to see whether there might have been a break-in, out of a curiosity which was not inborn but bred in training.

We gave them five minutes to get clear away then put the lights on again. I resumed my work. I picked up a couple of sacks from the pile beside the Fiat, carried them over to the lorry, and put them in the drum I had emptied. Then I replaced the lid and resealed it with new tape. Finally I hefted the full drum on to the lorry and manhandled it down to the space I had cleared at the front end of the box.

I kept emptying drums, filling them with heroin and resealing them until all the red bags had gone. By the time I had finished the sink was overflowing with bubbles and cleaner than it had been in thirty years. You even could see the cracks.

Now the heroin was packed neatly in the depths of the lorry. I emptied a last soap drum and loaded it with the empty polythene soap bags, then manoeuvered the drums around so that the heroin ones were hidden. I would know which drums contained heroin and which soap by the slightly different colour of the tape around the lids.

I closed the tailgate and locked it. Guy was just finishing re-assembling the Fiat. It looked perfect except for the upholstery, which was ruined.

I said: "I want you to take the Fiat back to the hire company. Park it outside their office and leave a note apologising for the damage plus enough money to pay for it.

"Drive the Citroen to England, and meet me at

6 p.m. tomorrow in the Dive Bar of the Lancaster Gate Hotel in Park Lane."

Guy said: "Are you sure you don't want me to drive the truck?"

I looked at him. "You must be nuts," I said. "Do you realise how long the police of either country would jail you for if you got your collar felt?"

He gave his to-hell-with-it grin. "I'm in this for adventure, remember? Besides, I don't want you to panic and balls it all up when we've got so far."

I winced at the implied reference to my blue funk performance in the lay-by incident. "I won't," I said dismissively. "How are you off for cash?"

"I'm all right for francs, but I need some limey money."

I gave him a handful of bills. While he was tightening the last few bolts on the Fiat I got my cases out of the Citroen and changed my clothes. I took off my bottle-green suit, now covered with detergent and completely ruined, and put on jeans. boots, a Levi jacket and a cap.

I took my sunglasses out of the car and put them on the dashboard shelf in the cab of the lorry. Guy handed me the export papers for the dishwasher powder and they went in the same place.

I turned out the garage lights and switched off the tap, then opened the door. Guy reversed the Fiat out.

I kicked over the engine of the lorry. It came to life instantly with a shattering roar. The fuel tank was full, the battery charging well, and the pressure in the air brakes high. I released the handbrake, wrenched the gear lever into first, revved the engine and inched forward. I was using the side lights only, not to draw attention—although the noise of the engine seemed enough to waken the dead.

I pulled out on to the road and switched on the headlights. I had never driven a lorry before, and a wet dark night in a strange country is neither the time nor the place to learn. I left Guy to close up the garage, and nursed the juggernaut around the first bend.

Dawn was breaking as I got to the coast. I soon had mastered the lorry. The main problems were getting an idea of the length of the thing, and taking corners wide enough to prevent the back wheels climbing the kerb. But the empty roads helped. I stopped at the dock to wait for the ferry.

My left leg ached from the strain of pressing down on the lorry's stiff clutch. But the ache in my belly was worse. When I thought about it I realised I hadn't eaten for twenty-four hours. But I was reluctant to leave the lorry to buy food. I decided to try to sleep—I had been without that for a day, too—but it seemed I was far too tense. I was sitting on a bomb, and it was hard to relax.

The cab had a radio, and I fiddled with the tuner for a while. All I could get was supermarket music or the news in Dutch. I settled for the music, and lay back in my seat with my eyes closed.

A loud banging on the door of the cab woke me. A uniformed official was shouting at me in French and pointing. My heart missed several guilty beats, and for the third time in twenty-four hours I thought I had met my cumuppance. Then I looked in the direction he was pointing. The ferry was in and I was holding up the queue.

I drove to the checkpoint where another official looked at my papers and waved me on. I drove on to the boat.

I slept again during the crossing, although I had no reason to feel secure. I still had a long way to go. When I woke up I felt worse.

The Customs were more thorough on the British side. They looked at my papers and asked me to open the tailgate. One of them took the lid off a soap drum and looked inside. But I think they were more worried about illegal immigrants than drugs. They okayed me.

I was in.

I put my foot down once I got on to the London road. The sky was clear after yesterday's rain, although there was a little early-morning mist about. The lorry cruised at 65 m.p.h. on the motorway.

When I reached London I went under the Blackwell Tunnel to the City office of one of my property companies. I stuck the lorry in the office car park.

The manager was most surprised to see me, especially in lorry-driver's clothes. "Well, Mr. Carstairs, well," he said nervously. "What can we do for you?" I had a reputation for instant firings, and no doubt he wondered whether he was in line for one. He was competent but idle, so I had two options: sack him or find some way of keeping him on his toes. Unexpected visits were a good way of keeping him on his toes. But I had no time to inspect the troops just now.

I said: "Is No. 17 Crown Terrace still vacant?"

"Why, yes, indeed."

I interrupted him. "Take it off the market. I've got new plans for it. And let me have the keys for it, please."

With a lot of yessirring the keys were found and brought. I noticed that the staff were almost as frightened of the manager as he was of me. I said: "Have I got the garage key here?"

"Oh, yes Mr. Carstairs, it's this one," purred the manager, grateful to have done something right.

I left him wiping his brow as I returned to the lorry. I half-expected it to be surrounded by police, peering in the cab and poking the tyres with sticks. But there was not a bluebottle in sight. I drove off.

Crown Terrace is an old street in the East End. Most of the property has been turned into small factories and beat-up offices or left empty to rot. No. 17 I had bought in a package, and I hadn't been able to do anything with it. Now it was coming into its own. There was a small garage in what had once been the garden. It was reached by a back lane. I drove down the lane and stopped the lorry at the back of No. 17.

I opened the garage door and the tailgate of the lorry, and with a weary sigh I began unloading again.

In half an hour the drums of heroin were stacked in the garage. I locked up and closed the tailgate of the lorry. Then I drove a few streets away to Sam Green's scrap-yard.

I had known Sam since my boyhood. I had done odd jobs for him in the yard for pennies and ha'pennies, and it hadn't taken me long to see that the yard was no more than a cover for all sorts of more profitable, less legal operations.

As a struggling young business man trying to get a builder's merchant's business off the ground, I had found Sam could supply all sorts of materials at low prices if no questions were asked.

Nowadays we saw each other only occasionally, and did no more business than a few pints and a hand of poker.

I found him in a corrugated iron hut smoking a hand-rolled cigarette and reading *The Sun*.

"Can you get rid of a lorry for me?" I asked him without preamble.

"Hot, is it?" he asked.

"Sort of."

"How much do you want?"

"You can have it for the favour of taking it off my hands."

"That hot, is it?"

"No, but I just don't want it to be traced back to me."

"Yes, all right, lad."

"There's a load of washing powder in the back. Give it to your missus," I added. Then I went.

I walked to a main road and waited five minutes for a cab. I gave the driver the address of my flat.

I sat back in the familiar surroundings of a London taxi and breathed easier.

I had made it.

Four hours later, shaved, bathed, dressed in a dark blue suit, and still desperately tired, I sat in the Dive Bar with a very large Scotch in my hand. Guy was late, but I wasn't worried. He had the safe end of the job.

I felt the Scotch filter into my bloodstream and relax me. The bar was almost empty, and I sat back in a comfortable chair and enjoyed the feeling of release. I had bought a late edition of the *Evening News* in the street. When I had finished the crossword and read the comic strips and the City Page I glanced at the news. Suddenly a story caught my eye. It was headlined: "Mystery man in car death riddle."

My jubilation drained as I read:

Police today were trying to solve the puzzle of a young man who died in a road accident on the A2 in Kent.

They are unable to identify the man, who was travelling alone in a white Citroen. And a senior detective said: "There are a number of unexplained factors about the crash."

The car is thought to be foreign because it has left-hand drive. The number plates were destroyed in the crash.

Police said there was no indication of the cause of the crash, which occurred in the early hours of today and did not involve any other vehicles.

But the biggest mystery lies in the state of the car. It had been dismantled partly either before or after the crash. The seats had been slashed and a number of parts removed.

The Kent police are anxious to hear from anyone who witnessed the crash or saw a white

Citroen in the Dartford area last night.

There was no room for doubt. The dead man was Guy. I left the paper on the bar and stumbled out into the rush hour.

CHAPTER FOURTEEN

I had expected Guy to get to England before me. He probably had passed me on the road out of Paris. He must have caught an earlier ferry, then been waylaid on the way to London.

The H gang must have forced him to crash. They probably hadn't intended to kill him—but they wouldn't be too bothered about it if they did. How they had got on to the Citroen I had no idea—but it showed me what a big league I was playing in.

I found myself at Marble Arch, and went down the Underground. At this time of day the Tube was quicker than a taxi. As I pushed my way through the crowds I looked at the faces of the people hurrying past me, and wished my worries were as small as theirs.

I bought a ticket and went down the escalator, speculating about my fellow commuters. Maybe that girl had stolen a stapler from the office, and was wondering about whether it would be missed. That man in a bowler might have risked a few hundred in a stock market flutter which was going wrong; perhaps that young man's girl had missed a period and he was afraid she was pregnant.

The dismantled car was the clincher. There could be only one reason for that: they had to be looking for the dope. Hell, they must be really close behind me. And so would the police be, soon. There were bound to be some identifying marks on the car: engine number, chassis number. The car would be traced through the manufacturers to the hire company in Paris, who would have all the details from my international driving licence, including my name and my London address. I had very little time left.

The carriage was unbearably stuffy. I had literally to shoulder my way in. There was no need to strap-hang, because we were packed so tight there was no room to fall over.

I could see my own reflection in the window as the train raced into the tunnel. I saw a well-dressed man in his forties with chin-length grey hair. There were heavy worry-lines around the eyes, and the downturned moustache gave the face a permanently grim expression.

You have plenty to look grim about, chum, I thought. You have committed most serious crimes in two countries, you have spent a small fortune on dangerous drugs, and you have the most powerful criminal organisation in the country thirsting for your blood. Not to mention the fact that you have put your business reputation at risk by misusing a large loan from a highly-respectable bank.

Richard Elliott would go mad when he learned I had spent the money he raised for a plum building site on an unprofitable fleet of lorries.

I got off at my stop and walked up to street level. If I were Mr. H, I thought, what would I do next? It would depend on how much I knew. Well, where Mr. H. was getting his information was a mystery, but it seemed my efforts to cover my tracks had failed. At the worst, the hosts of the ungodly might even know who I was and where I lived.

The flat was no longer safe, I decided. I would ask the girls to take a holiday in my cottage in Wales, and I would move into an hotel.

As I hurried along the pavement I nervously scanned the faces of the other pedestrians, expecting each of them to suddenly pull a gun and hustle me into a car. I saw a rare beat bobby a few yards in front of me, and kept close to him until he turned off my route. Then I told myself to quit acting like a scared kitten.

I met Annabel outside our block. She just was coming home from the studio.

"I made it," I told her. "But Guy House—the American who was working for me—they got him. He was ambushed on the way back. He's dead."

Her big blue eyes got even wider. "Dead!" she whispered.

I nodded grimly as we got into the lift. "They are closer to me than I imagined," I said. "We've got to make new plans."

Annabel was too frightened to be angry. Her face was white and she turned away from me to face the blank wall of the lift. "Apples, what have you got into?"

"God knows." We walked along the corridor to

112

our door. "For starters I want us all to move out of the flat," I said. Annabel opened the door and stopped so suddenly I bumped into her back.

"Too late," she said flatly.

I looked past her. In the hall the carpet had been pulled up and the pictures from the wall lay scattered on the floor. I pushed past Annabel and walked through the open living room door.

The carpet was up there, too, and all the furniture had been ripped to shreds. The units had been smashed up, the bookshelves emptied, the television and the hi-fi broken open.

Every room in the house was the same. Everything that might have hidden something had been smashed, ripped, broken. The freezer had been emptied and the food was defrosting in a puddle on the kitchen floor. The lid on the w.c. in the bathroom had been taken off and dropped into the bath, where it had smashed. In the bedroom the duvet and the mattress had been slashed and all the stuffing pulled out. Each of our three small studies had been worked over thoroughly.

I came back into the living room and contemplated the shambles of my home. I picked up my Picasso original from the floor. "They weren't thieves," I told Annabel, showing her the picture. "They didn't bother to take this. It's worth a six-figure sum on its own." Then I dropped it uncaringly on the floor.

Annabel was looking around, dazed. She had not moved since she entered the living room. Now she stood motionless in the doorway, a look of blank horror on her finely-carved features.

"I wonder how they got in," I said inconsequentially. My eye lighted on something on the floor. It was a pair of panties I had bought Babs. On the front was embroidered the slogan: "End race hate—miscegenate." A bell rang in the back of my mind. The same bell tolled its alarm in Annabel's mind, triggered by my idle question. Together we both gasped: "Babs!"

I did not want to believe she might be in the hands of those vicious bastards. Perhaps she hadn't got home yet—maybe they broke in, or conned the janitor.

But maybe they didn't—maybe they just rang the bell and Babs answered the door. How could I tell? Frantically I searched my mind and the jumble of wreckage on the floor. Then I turned over the panties in my hand, and got my answer.

On the back, written in block capitals with a felt pen, were the words: "We got your nig nog tart. Wait by the phone and you may see her alive again."

I handed the message to Annabel. She read it, and snapped out of her daze. "Apples, we must get her back."

I slumped in a chair, my face buried in my hands. For the first time since my childhood I felt the force of tears pushing urgently at the back of my eyeballs. "The best thing might be to wait by the phone like they said," I muttered. I wanted nothing now but the chance to admit defeat, sue for peace, and get back to normal, happy living.

"What will they be doing to her while we wait?" Annabel replied angrily. "You know what happened last time! She got raped—three times—and you know what a repeat of that could do to the girl's emotions."

I knew. In some ways Babs was emotionally fragile. If it had been Annabel who had been kidnapped I would have worried a lot less. She would know how to handle a rape scene—she might even have enjoyed it. Babs was totally different. She hated aggressive love-making, and we were always very gentle with each other. Annabel and I could get mildly sadistic with one another if the mood took us, but never with Babs. I suppose it was because of her childhood experience.

If she were raped again it could shatter the brittle structure of independence she had built up in a year with Annabel and me.

Annabel stood in front of me and gripped me by the shoulders. "Apples, think hard," she said urgently. "Where could they have taken her?"

I shook my head. "Hell, I don't know enough about them." Then I mentally shook myself and started thinking. "It wouldn't be the Sloane Square flat," I said. "That is too valuable to them as a safe house. The only other place I can think of is that club—the Purple End. But I doubt . . ."

Annabel had turned away and already was striding out of the door. She called over her shoulder: "We'll take my car." I followed, slamming the door behind me.

She drove the blue Ferrari with fierce skill. She didn't get out of second gear all the way to Leicester Square. She parked smack outside the club on a double yellow line. Before getting out, she reached into the glove box and pulled out a small pistol.

I gaped. "Can you use that?" I asked incredulously.

"Yes," she said curtly, slipping it into the breast pocket of her Levi jacket. She opened the boot and took out a heavy adjustable spanner. "Put that in your pocket," she told me. I complied obediently, happy to let her give the orders while she was doing so well.

The door to the club was open. It was about eight o'clock, and a roadie was carrying the group's equipment in from a van ready for the night's cacophonous performance.

Annabel went in behind the roadie. As she started down the steps, the burly doorman appeared behind her.

"What do you want?" he said rudely. I dislike people who are discourteous to my women. I came up behind him and hit the back of his head with my spanner, throwing all of my weight into the blow. He sagged, and I caught him and shoved him into the corner. I shouted to Annabel: "Go!"

I rand down the stone steps after her, pushing past the roadie. Inside the club, one or two people standing at the bar looked on with mild interest as we ran across the dance floor to the door at the side of the stage marked "Private". We ran down a short corridor and burst through another door marked "Office".

The man sitting behind the desk looked up, startled. He was a negro with short hair and broad shoulders, and he wore a dinner jacket and black bow tie with a white ruffled shirt.

The pistol was in Annabel's hand. The man put his hands out in front of him in a protective gesture. Without preamble Annabel said: "Where is the girl?"

"Hey, I don't know what you're talking about, honest to Jesus I don't. I ain't the manager, I'm just looking after the place for a few hours tonight, it's the truth."

"Where's the manager?" I asked him.

"I don't know."

I took a quick step forward and swung at him with the spanner. It smashed into his mouth, breaking a couple of teeth. He yelped with pain and put his hands to his bleeding face.

"Where is the manager?" I repeated.

"He told me he was going to Reading," the man said through a mouthful of blood. "He asked me to look after the place until he comes back. He's coming back after midnight. He didn't tell where he was going. He didn't tell me there would be trouble. Jesus, please believe me."

I lifted the spanner again. "No," Annabel said. "He's telling the truth. Let's go."

We ran out of the office and across the club again. As we got to the exit the door opened and the doorman stepped through. I hit him again with the spanner. It wasn't his lucky day.

Some of the others in the club realised what was happening then. A woman screamed, there were a couple of shouts from the men at the bar, and some of the men came after us as we mounted the steps to the street door.

We pushed past the roadie struggling down the stairs with a hefty amplifier. As I passed him I gave him a push from behind. He and the amp went tumbling down the steps on top of our pursuers. We ran out of the club and jumped into the car.

As we tore down the road I said: "Where next?"

"Alastair John," she replied.

"I doubt if he'll be any help," I mused. "I'm pretty sure he's not in this end of the racket. Oh, I know he's a pusher, but I think he's got scruples. Besides, I've known him a long time. I think we might have done better to lean on the black in the club a little harder."

"We had no time," Annabel said. "While it was two of us against one of him we were all right. But a few more seconds and someone else would have come in. Then we would have found it much more difficult to get out."

She jumped a set of lights and cornered sharply with a scream of tyres. "I know Al is a long shot," she went on. "But even if he isn't directly involved he may have heard something. He keeps his ear to the ground. Anyway, he's the only lead we have."

And that was true, I thought, as we screeched to a stop outside the little house in Chelsea. We ran up to the door and I leaned on the bell-push until the door was opened by a man I did not know.

I pushed past him into the hall. "Where's Al?" I asked brusquely.

"Charmed, I'm sure," the man said. "Is it against your religion to say hello?"

I had no time to fence words with this little poof. I caught hold of his shirt-front and swung him around against the wall. His head rocked back on his neck and smashed the glass in a picture frame.

"Where's Al?" I asked again.

His cockiness did a disappearing trick. "Gone to Reading," he said quickly.

I released him and looked at Annabel. "Reading again," I said.

I heard the sound of a telephone dial and swung around to the poof. He was dialling 999. I pushed him away and ripped the phone cable cable out of the wall. Then I turned back to Annabel.

"Just a minute," she said. "I'm trying to think."

Suddenly something crashed against the back of my skull. I turned around again, to see the poof, with a terrified expression on his face, wielding the telephone handset like a club. I grabbed his wrist.

"Will you for Chrissake stop playing at cops and robbers?" I said. "This is for real." I gave him another push and he went flying.

"I've got it!" Annabel said triumphantly.

"Well?" But she was gone.

I jumped into the car beside her just as she let out the clutch with a stomach-wrenching jerk. When I had recovered from the Houston-style take-off I said: "Reading is a big place. Where do we start looking?"

"Remember Johnny Robins? His country house is outside Reading."

I thought about that as I rolled around in the bucket seat. It was a good guess. Where better to keep a prisoner than a remote mansion in its own grounds? We knew Robins was mixed up in all this. Of course, he wouldn't like his place used as a dungeon, but he was in so deep the gang must have a strong hold on him. I didn't quite see how Al was tied in—but maybe his was just a social visit.

It was worth a try. Besides, it was the only lead we had.

As we hit the motorway Annabel changed into third gear at 75 m.p.h. I put on my seat belt.

After about 20 minutes we turned off. Annabel's Ferrari was superb on the motorway, but it really came into its own on a road with a bit of character. It blew past other cars like a gust of wind, and cornered like it was glued to the tarmac. Annabel knew just how far she could push it, and she drove it to the limit.

There was a nasty moment when we swept around a bend and found ourselves almost on top of a slow lorry with no room to overtake. My heart leaped into my mouth. Annabel trod hard on the power brakes, and it was as if a giant hand snatched the car's lithe body and gently but relentlessly brought it to a halt. Because of the seat belt, I didn't even crack my head on the windscreen.

Soon after that Annabel pulled off the road on to a grass verge beside a high wall. "I used to come here in my debutante days," she said with a wry smile. She despised the shallow social life led by many rich men's daughters, and her contempt was all the more profound because she had once enjoyed that sort of life herself. She went on: "If I remember rightly, you can see the house from the top of this wall."

I climbed out of the car. A small tree grew beside the wall a few yards away, and I grabbed a low branch and hauled myself up like a monkey.

"Well?" Annabel called.

"We won't have to worry about how we're going to get in," I called back.

Across about half a mile of fields I could see the house. It was a small stately home, about two hundred years old. I guessed it had about 25 bedrooms. Light poured from dozens of windows, distant music floated over the fields, and the drive and forecourt were crammed with Rolls-Royces, Jaguars, Mercedes and Volvos. The St. Clair Robinses were having a party.

I jumped down from the tree and got back into the car. "There's a big do of some kind on there," I told Annabel. "The Hunt Ball or something, I shouldn't wonder. We can gate-crash it."

"What about our clothes?" she said.

She had a point. We couldn't burst in and hold a couple of hundred people up at gunpoint. We would have to pose as guests. I was still in my dark blue suit, so I could pass muster even if it was a dinner-jacket affair. But Annabel still had on her denims and sandals.

"Hold on," I said. I unbuttoned her jacket and held it aside.

"This is not time for . . ."

"I know," I interrupted her. "I'm not doing this just for the pleasure of gazing at your mammoth mammaries. How long is that shirt?"

"It comes about an inch below the pubes."

"Has it got a shirt-tail?"

"No, it's straight."

"Have you got your knickers on?"

"Under Levis? Sure to."

"That's it, then. Your shirt is a dress. Whip off your trousers and jacket, and you're okay."

"If this weren't so bloody serious, I'd think you were doing it out of lechery," she said. But she took them off.

She smoothed out the creases in the bottom of her shirt and started the engine. A few hundred yards farther along the road we came to the entrance. We pulled on to the gravel and passed between two large, ugly stone lions, covered with moss and bird-shit, which guarded the Robins estate. Tall trees stood at attention along the drive. The Ferrari screeched to a stop in front of the house.

"Turn the car around," I suggested. Annabel looked at me. "For a quick getaway," I added. She did a fast three-point turn.

We left the keys in the ignition and the doors unlocked. The house was pretty big, and in good condition. I was impressed: Robins had done well for a wine merchant, I thought. Then I remembered he had other sources of income.

I felt a bit sheepish walking up the weathered stone steps to the grand doorway which you could have driven a bus through. Annabel looked like a clothes horse and my jacket, which was cut to fit very closely, bulged inelegantly with a big spanner and a small gun.

But as we stepped into the brightly-lit hall a transformation came over Annabel. She straightened up, her eyes flashing haughtily, and suddenly her shirt looked like a Paris original and her sandals just the right choice to go with it.

The butler stepped forward, making me wish I had a hat to hand him. Instead I said: "Mr. Chadwell Carstairs and Lady Annabel Dath, but please don't announce us as we're so late."

"Very good, sir," he said, and melted away. We hurried toward the ballroom in order to disappear in the crowd as quickly as possible. No such luck.

The ballroom door opened in front of us and out stepped Robins.

CHAPTER FIFTEEN

I was dumbstruck for a second or two.

A slightly puzzled smile came over Robins face. "Hello, my dear," he said to Annabel.

I stuck out my hand. "How are you, Robins, jolly nice of you to invite us. You've probably forgotten, you were pretty well sloshed at old Alastair's party."

"Not at all," he lied, the puzzled expression vanishing quickly from his eyes. "Al's here somewhere. Good party, his was, what?" He looked slightly embarrassed. " 'Fraid this one won't be quite so exotic. Come on in, have a good time." He ushered us into the ballroom and passed on.

I breathed a quiet sigh of relief and looked around the room. A small orchestra played on a stage on the far side, their dreary music muffled by the two-hundred-odd bodies between us and them. There was the inevitable buffet table along one wall, and waiters moved around the crowd with trays of glasses. The roar of conversation enabled

Annabel and me to talk to each other without being overheard.

"What does that mean?" Annabel said, jerking a thumb to the doorway where we had left Robins. "That Babs isn't here?"

"That's one possibility," I said. "The second possibility is that Robins is a very good actor. And the third is that Robins knows she's here but doesn't know who she is or why she's been snatched. After all, he's never met her. If the gang didn't put him in the picture then he has no idea she's connected with us."

We proceeded to mingle, nodding at one or two people and snatching glasses of champagne from passing waiters. Some of the guests wore evening dress, but as many wore lounge suits, and there were a few youngsters in gaudy tie-less oufits, so we did not look conspicuous.

"Let's have a look around the house," I said after a while. Two grand sets of stairs ran up from each side of the ballroom. No doubt they led to the first floor of the east and west wings respectively. The ballroom occupied the whole depth and height of the house where the two wings met.

"All right," said Annabel. "You take the east wing. We'll do the upstairs first and meet back at the bar in fifteen minutes." We split up.

There was quite a lot of traffic on the stairs, as they led to the bathrooms. As I mounted the carpeted steps I saw the back of a familiar head a few stairs ahead of me. It was Alastair. I quickened my pace and followed him.

At the top of the stairs he turned into the bathroom. I went in after him. Apart from the two of us it was empty, but it might not stay that way for long. I grabbed him roughly from behind and shoved him into the w.c. cubicle. I released him and locked the door.

He turned around. "Chadwell! What the hell . . ."

"Sit down," I snarled, and cut him short by pushing him on to the seat of the toilet. I pulled out the pistol and pointed it at him. He whitened.

"I'm going to ask you one fucking question, Al," I said in a low voice. "If you lie to me I'll kill you."

"Chadwell, is this some kind . . . "

"Shut up. Are you here on business or pleasure?"

He looked me straight in the eye and said: "Pleasure. But—"

"Right." I pulled back the safety catch on the pistol, leaned back against the door, and pointed the gun straight between his eyes.

He started to laugh. He closed his eyes and rocked backward and forward on the toilet seat giggling. Suddenly I saw the funny side of it. Here I was, standing in a bog with the biggest queer in London, pointing a pistol at his head, and he was laughing. I laughed too.

His reactions had convinced me he wasn't in on whatever was happening to Babs. If he had been, he couldn't possibly have laughed, for he would then have known I meant business. and no one, not even the greatest actor, can look death in the face and laugh.

His giggling subsided and I sobered quickly. "I'm sorry, Al, but this is serious," I said. "I can't explain it right now, but just don't tell a soul about this incident tonight."

"Darling, could I tell the world I'd been in a toilet with Apples Carstairs and failed to seduce him? I'd never live it down."

I turned, opened the door, and went out. There was a man washing his hands at the basin, and the look on his face when he saw Al walk out of the cubicle after me was hilarious. Al noticed, and had to compound the folly by putting his arm around me as we walked out of the door and saying: "Thank you, darling, that was gorgeous." I just hoped I would never meet the hand-washer again.

Outside the door we went different ways: Al back to the ballroom and me along the corridor. I turned a right-angled bend and walked quickly to the end of the wing. Then I started trying doors.

Most were open, and led to empty bedrooms. One room was a nursery. It was darkened, and I could see twin beds with small children asleep in them. Ah well, I thought, even villains have kids.

Some more empty rooms, then a locked door. I listened for a moment. On the other side I could hear heavy breathing, then a low moan. I recognized it · instantly as the sound made by a woman being nicely screwed.

In another bedroom I surprised a woman adjusting her corset. Her heavy breasts nearly popped out of the elastic armour when she saw my face poking around the door. She squealed, and I said: "Beg pardon—looking for the gents" and quickly slammed the door.

That was the lot. I made my way back to the bar, where Annabel was waiting for me. She looked at me questioningly. "Nothing," I said.

"Me too."

"Oh, I did meet Alastair. I pointed the gun at him and asked him if he was here on business. He laughed. I'm pretty sure his presence here is a coincidence."

"If you say so. Ground floor next?"

"Yes. Same plan?"

"Right. My side is the servants' quarters and the kitchens. Yours is where the family live. Fifteen minutes."

I went through a door behind the staircase. It led to a series of dining rooms and reception rooms. One or two people were wandering around looking at the oil paintings and antique furniture bought, I reminded myself, with the profits made from lingering death. Most of the doors were open. I tried a couple that weren't, and found a study and a playroom. Then I made my way back.

This time I beat Annabel to it. A couple of minutes later she arrived. In the meantime I had organized a couple of Scotches—the champagne was a bit feeble for this sort of work.

She took a swallow of the neat whisky. "Nothing on this floor," she said. "I got questioned by a man-servant on the way, but I made up some story about wanting to look at the kitchens."

"It looks as if we've drawn a blank," I said morosely. Our initial frantic haste had been dispelled by the nitty-gritty of searching and pretending to be partygoers, and now we both felt a little helpless.

"There's one more possibility," Annabel said. "Just outside the door to the ground floor of the west wing there was a narrow flight of stairs leading down. Perhaps there's a basement."

"Right." I downed the rest of my drink, feeling galvanised into action again. We went out to the west wing. Just the other side of the door, on the right-hand side, there was a spiral staircase. We slipped down it quickly.

At the foot of the stairs was a door. I opened it.

We found ourselves in a big room with white-washed walls. Strip lights in the low ceiling shed a bright illumination. There was a full-size ping-pong table, a billiards table, and a couple of card tables. In a corner was a glass chess table with a delicately carved set of pieces on it.

Across the room were two more doors. The first led to a wall cupboard full of games. The second was locked.

I looked again at the second door. It had a padded surface. "Looks like a soundproofed music room," Annabel speculated. Sure enough, when I thought about it. I could hear the sound of an orchestra on the other side of the door.

"You're right," I said. "There's a record playing."

While I was wondering what to do next the handle of the door turned. We both sprang back instinctively. The door opened outward, concealing us from whoever was coming through it.

As the door swung to again I saw the back of a tall, smartly-dressed black man wearing tight leather trousers and a bowler hat. It was unmistakably Harry Hat. I reached forward, tipped the bowler over his eyes with my left hand, and swung the spanner in my right. I was getting handy with the spanner, and my blow caught him squarely and powerfully on the crown of his head.

The ear-splitting blast of music from the room drowned any sound he may have made as he fell to the floor like a dropped puppet. I handed Annabel the gun and we stepped into the room.

The scene made my stomach turn over. Babs was lying on the floor, naked and tied up. Her head was nearest us, and standing behind it with his back to us was a man. Her legs were tied to the feet of a table, and kneeling in front of the table and between her knees was a second man. He had the mad grin of a sadist on his face, and in his hand was a smoking cigarette. I could see burn marks on Babs' thigh, making a track upwards, and the tears on her face tracked down. Her mouth was opened in a scream, but the sound was drowned by the noise of Beethoven's Ninth blasting from two huge speakers on the floor.

The torturer lifted the cigarette to his lips to puff more life into it. As he raised his head he saw us, and his jaw dropped.

Suddenly a bloody stain appeared on the back of the standing man. Some remote part of my brain registered that Annabel must have shot him, although I didn't hear the bang. The rest of my mind was possessed by a terrible hatred. I leaped at the kneeling man, swinging the spanner.

The wild blow ripped a gash in his cheek but he got to his feet and punched me. The blow landed on the bridge of my nose. I felt nothing. I swung again, catching him on the jaw. He fell back on the table. I lifted the spanner high and brought it down on the top of his head. He fell backward farther and his head banged down on the table. I lifted the spanner above my head and brought it down in the middle of his face. His nose gushed blood. I brought the spanner down again and again in his face, my right arm a mindless machine operated by blind, consuming rage. Suddenly the music stopped.

I realised the man on the table had not moved for some time. I stopped hitting him. His face was a mass of bleeding flesh, hardly recognisable as human.

I turned. Annabel was untying Babs, who was whimpering softly. I went into the games room and dragged the still body of Harry Hat back into the music room. I hit his head again to make sure he stayed unconscious, then I locked the door. It would give us some extra, precious seconds.

Annabel had untied Babs and they were in each other's arms, crying. I strode past them and opened the far door. It led to a cellar. The place obviously once had been used to store coal, but now it was full of gardening tools. It was relatively clean, which meant it was still in use. And since they would hardly carry wheelbarrows and shovels through the music room, that meant there was another entrance.

I looked around. In a corner was a steep wooden open staircase, with no handrail, which led to a door at ceiling level. I tried to remember my brief glance at the outside of the house. I thought there had been a doorway tucked in an angle of the brickwork on the east side of the main entrance. It figured—the basement started on the west side, ran under the big entrance hall and came out on the east side. Yes, I could remember a door in the side of the front steps. I went back into the music room.

Annabel was helping Babs into her clothes. I

said: "There's a way out through here."

Annabel looked up. "Okay," she said. "Just a minute."

"Hurry," I said. "We don't know how long it will be before someone gets suspicious and comes down here to check."

"Not long at all," came a cultured voice from behind me. I spun around then froze. Robins stood in the doorway to the cellar. Out of the elegant sleeve of his dinner jacket there stuck a spotless white cuff; out of the cuff stuck a finely manicured hand, and out of the hand stuck a snub-nosed pistol.

He looked at the two bodies. He grimaced at the bloody face of the man on the table. "You have made a mess of poor Hollingbery," he drawled. "I doubt if they'll want him for the centrefold of Cosmopolitan now. And old Parrish bought his, too, I see. You have been busy."

As I suspected, the two we had killed were only small fry, I thought. But I had underestimated Robins. How high in the organisation was he? I doubted if he could be my Mr. H.—whoever bossed this organisation would steer well clear of anything as overtly criminal as kidnapping.

Robins was smart to have caught us, but I still did not think he was all that bright. He was looking pleased with himself now, instead of worrying about what he was going to do next.

I wondered whether he knew of the tie-up between me, Babs and the heroin gang. Then he started to answer my unvoiced questions.

"Fancy you two being mixed up in all this," he said. "I thought I hadn't invited you here. It's as well I came down to check on things and saw Harry's bowler lying all forlorn on the floor of the games room." I cursed myself for my carelessness in leaving it there.

He went on: "Before you start thinking about indulging in any more heroics, like escaping, I might as well tell you I've got several chaps outside, ah, keeping an eye on the cars and whatnot. You wouldn't get far."

He was standing beside one of the heavy three-foot stereo speakers. I was leaning on the amplifier, and while he was shooting off his mouth I was surreptitiously turning the balance control right round. When I gently pressed the piano-key switch which restarted the record, a blast of music like an explosion came out of the speaker beside Robins.

He started, and half turned. It was all I needed. The spanner flew from my hand at his head. But it was a long time since I had played cricket, and it only grazed his temple. I dived to one side as he fired. Then he slumped sideways. Annabel had been more accurate than I.

I turned the music off again and looked at Robins. The bullet had taken him in the abdomen. He probably would live.

"Quick!" I said. The women followed me into the cellar.

"I'll go first," I said. "I'll get in the car and get it started. With luck no one will question me. I'll drive up beside the door and blow the horn. Then you two come out and dive into the car."

Annabel nodded. Babs did and said nothing, but gazed straight ahead with a blank look in her eyes.

I climbed the stairs and gently opened the

wooden door. It was completely dark now, but the house and the area around it were bathed in light from lamps and spotlights. I strolled across the gravel and slid behind the wheel of the Ferrari. I noticed a man watching me idly from the drive. I turned the key and the engine leaped to life instantly. Unhurriedly, I reversed up to the door in the steps.

When I sounded a long, raucous blast on the horn the watching man suddenly got interested. He started running toward us. I opened the passenger door and flung the front seat forward. In the next second Babs and Annabel fell into the back seat of the car. I had the gears in first and my foot on the clutch ready. I touched the accelerator and released the clutch with a jerk.

The car's fat radials spun on the gravel then bit. It shot forward like a bullet from a gun. I swung the wheel and aimed it straight down the drive. The man who had been running at us suddenly dived to one side out of the way.

I threw a switch that turned on the headlights and changed into second gear. The trees flashed by in a continuous blur. We were doing sixty miles an hour down the half-mile drive when the headlights of another car turned in through the entrance. The drive was long, but narrow, and as the car got rapidly closer I saw that there was hardly room for us to pass one another between the rows of trees. I stamped on the brakes.

The other car—I could see now it was a wide Mercedes Pulman—came to a stop. I was almost on top of it, and still travelling fast, when I spun the wheel. We skidded sideways. I released the brake and stamped on the accelerator and we shot out between a gap in the avenue of trees.

I spun the wheel again, the opposite way, gouging great chunks out of Robins' fitted-carpet lawn, and shot back on to the drive on the other side of the Mercedes. I caught a brief glimpse of the faces in the car as my headlights flashed across its windows: their expressions frozen in almost comical looks of amazement and fright.

We passed the stone lions again and got on to the road. I considered the possibility of pursuit for a moment. It would take them a while to get organised, and I hadn't seen a car there that could get anywhere near the Ferrari for speed. Besides, they had no idea where we would go. I decided we were safe for the moment.

I stopped the car in a village not far from the motorway and went into a phone box. I looked at my watch. It was a couple of minutes past midnight. I dialled the office of my old paper. I had a debt to repay.

Jack McIntyre was still there, working very late. I told him: "I haven't got much time, Jack. Don't ask how I know, and don't for God's sake say I told you, but there's been a double murder at John Robins' country house near Reading. Robins himself is wounded, maybe dead."

"How long ago, Apples?" he said.

"Minutes," I replied. "You've got it all to yourself for the one o'clock edition." I hung up.

Back in the car Babs was asleep, curled up in Annabel's arms. As we moved off I said: "How is she?"

"It's difficult to tell. I don't think the burns are

134

too bad, but the shock may be something else."

We were silent for a while then. After we had been on the motorway for a quarter of an hour Annabel realised we were heading west, instead of going east back to London.

"Where are we going?" she said.

I replied: "To the seaside."

It was four a.m. when we reached the west coast of Wales. The headlights revealed a fine drizzle as I drove up the mud track to the old farmhouse.

I had bought the farm along with the farmhouse a couple of years ago. The house was about 100 years old, but I had practically rebuilt it. I had also put up a new bungalow a couple of miles away. That and the land was leased to a farmer. I did not charge them any rent—the land was so poor they could hardly have survived—but in return they kept an eye on the old place for me when it was empty.

I wearily clambered out of the car. I seemed to have been driving all my life. This was my second night without sleep. I unlocked the door and went in. .I switched on the lights and went into the kitchen. The boiler was made up and all ready to be lit. I opened the fire door and put a match to it. It would be a while before the fire warmed the place.

Annabel and Babs staggered in. I said: "Let's have a look at Babs' leg, then go to bed."

The burns were painful, and they would stay that way for a few days, but they did not come into the serious category. I found some ointment in the first aid box and Annabel constructed a light bandage.

While she was putting the dressing on I made up

the bed. It was a vast one, like the bed in the flat. I switched on the electric blanket to air it, then put on sheets and several blankets.

The women came upstairs and we fell into bed.

We awakened late the following afternoon. I still felt exhausted, Babs was d ained by the torture, and Annabel's supercool—which had stood us in such good stead the night before—had given way to a dejected apathy.

There were some tins of food in a cupboard in the kitchen. I made a pie with tinned meat, tinned vegetables, and instant potato. We sat around the pine kitchen table eating the meal in a desultory way and watching the relentless drizzle through the windows. Then we went back to bed and slept all night.

That night I had a nightmare. I was trying to light the boiler, but I kept dropping the matches. They were falling on Babs and kept burning her. Some men were creeping up the road to the farmhouse. One was wearing a hat which kept changing colour; another had a shapeless, bloody mess where his face should have been; and the third man's face was a white blank with a capital H on it. I had to get the boiler alight before they got to the farmhouse. Then, with a terrible shock, I realised the boiler was full of heroin and I could never light it. I threw the spanner at the man with the H on his face. Suddenly his face changed and I could see who it was. I yelled: "The Citroen! I should have known!" My own voice wakened me.

A bright, cold early morning sun was struggling

to warm the countryside. I could hear the noise of sheep quite close by. The air was sharp and chilly in my nostrils, but the bed was warm. Babs was fast asleep beside me, and on the other side of her Annabel was buried under the blankets. My cries obviously had not disturbed them.

I tried to remember the face I had seen momentarily in my dream, but it had gone in the ephemeral way dreams do. All I could remember was my utter amazement at the man's identity: the emotion lingered although the cause of it had gone.

Then I remembered the words I had shouted. The Citroen: what could be significant about the Citroen? And which Citroen had I been referring to? It could be either the black one which had abducted Guy or the white one in which Guy had met his death. But neither of them seemed to provide a clue.

I had the feeling I knew all I needed to figure out the identity of Mr. H., but although I had almost completed the jigsaw I could not see what the picture was until I placed the last piece.

I got out of bed and tiptoed shivering across the polished floorboards to the bathroom. The boiler had heated the water even if it had failed to warm the house. I ran a steaming hot bath and got in.

I lay back and let the warmth smooth out the last few creases left by the recent hassles. We had come out of it pretty well, I considered, when you think how low we got at one point. My biggest problem was that I still didn't know just how much Mr. H. knew about me. He obviously realised my jaunt to Marseilles was a once-only job. If I had been a regular supplier, he would have brought from me without a murmur. But as I was never going to be useful to him again, he would rather steal the dope from me and save himself a million pounds. I wondered whether he knew my precise motivation for setting up the deal. And whether he knew I would try to double-cross him.

He might feel differently about doing business with me now. I had managed to stay one jump ahead of him so far—although it was more by luck than by judgement. All the same, his attempts to double-cross me had led him into some sticky situations. He had murdered Guy—or at any rate his minions had—and God only knew what the result of the fracas at Robins' mansion would be: at the very least, Robins' usefulness was ended. Once a Minister had been involved in an underworld shoot-out he lost his greatest asset—that of being above suspicion.

Mr. H. by now might be ready to do business with me. I would let him stew for a few days.

I got out of the bath, dried myself, and started to shave. My face in the bathroom mirror bore no signs of strain. For a decadent middle-aged criminal, I told myself, you have remarkable powers of recovery.

In the big old chest of drawers on the landing I found heavy denim jeans—yer actual slimline Wranglers, none of this fancy flared rubbish—and a thick fisherman's roll-neck sweater. I tiptoed downstairs on the creaky staircase and got dressed. Just in case the women woke up before I got back, I scribbled them a note and put it on the kitchen table under the tea caddy. Then I put on the Wellington boots I kept in the outhouse and went out.

The air tasted better than draught lager. I climbed over a fence and stepped across the fileds. I felt so good-natured I even skirted the sheep to avoid bothering them.

On the far side of a rise I saw Cledwyn Price, the farmer. He was examining a couple of new lambs.

"Good ones, Mr. Price?" I called.

"Lovely strong creatures," he told me as I came up to him. "Every one a little miracle, God be thanked."

"Tasty, too, I expect," I said. He was a short, dark man, and very devout. He never asked questions about the relationship between Babs, Annabel and me, but he had dark suspicions. My conversations with him were always a little uneasy, as he would keep bringing God in in the persistent way Noncomformists have. He would have liked to disapprove of me, but he couldn't quite jusitfy it.

"We noticed your car," he said. "Mrs. Price came over yesterday midday, but there was no one about so she didn't disturb you." In that innocuous sentence was all the contempt of a man of the land for city types who lie in bed all day.

"That was thoughtful," I said. "Well, I'll go and see her now. I'm hoping she can let me have some supplies."

"Surely she will."

I waved to him and went on. The sun was drying the dew now, and the day looked like becoming hot. As I tramped over the fields I began to regret the thick sweater. I didn't hurry, and it took me another half an hour to reach the Prices' bungalow.

Mrs. Price was rather more jolly than her husband, and secretly took his strict Noncomformism with a pinch of salt. She had taken a shine to me from the start, and she thought the three of us were deliciously scandalous.

As I walked through the kitchen door I called: "Hello, Mrs. Price. Lovely morning, isn't it."

"Well, Mr. Carstairs," she said, pretending to be surprised. "There's nice weather it is for a little holiday for you. Would you like a cup of tea?"

"It's just what I need after that long walk. You know if this was London I would have taken a taxi."

"Don't be daft." She was warming up now, the formality disappearing fast. She poured the tea and I took a sip.

"Have you got any eggs for me, to build up my strength?" I said with a broad wink. She flushed and giggled.

"Now, none of your old nonsense in this house," she said with an attempt at severity which failed hopelessly.

I went out to the hen-house and collected a basket of eggs. When I went back into the bungalow Mrs. Price was at the oven. "Mmm, is that fresh bread I smell?" I said.

"You shall have some if you behave," she said. She was younger than I, but I don't think she knew it, and she liked to treat me as a mischievous lad.

I ended up with a dozen eggs, two new loaves, a big flask of milk still warm from the cow, and a bag of Welsh cakes. "And none of your old money, now," said Mrs. Price. "It all comes from your own land." This was a ritual we went through. I pretended to be on the cadge, she refused money, then I gave it to her by some subterfuge.

140

As I was leaving, I said: "Oh, Mrs. Price, has your husband killed any of those new lambs yet?"

With feigned exasperation she took a leg of lamb out of the fridge and added it to my basket. "It's protein for me, you see," I said with another wink.

"Go on with you now, before my husband come back and hears you talk so," she said, pushing me out of the house.

I waved her good-bye. When she went back into the kitchen she would find a fiver under the tea pot.

The sun was high and I was dripping with sweat by the time I got back to my place. I put the food away and went upstairs to wake the women.

Their sleeping faces were side by side on one pillow. A strand of blonde hair strayed across Annabel's pale skin and aquiline nose, and trembled in the breath from her open, mobile mouth. She was snoring. Babs' dark chocolate skin was almost as black as her thick hair, and there was a slight tremor of fear around her closed eyes as she breathed. I kissed them both gently.

Annabel stretched and yawned massively. "What a lovely day," she muttered blearily. Babs opened her eyes wide. Then she smiled at me and snuggled up to Annabel.

"I've walked five miles already," I said heartily. "How about that?"

"Masochist," said Annabel. Babs giggled.

"Being the healthy outdoor type, I will now cook breakfast," I said.

We had boiled eggs, fresh bread, and strong tea. Afterwards we ate some of the Welsh cakes. I sat back with a cigarette and a fresh cup of tea.

"You can keep your filet mignon and your duck

a l'orange," I said with a satisfied smile.

"You wouldn't say that if you had to eat eggs every day, Babs said.

"Most days I can't face cornflakes in the morning, let alone eggs," said Annabel. "It must be something to do with the air."

After a while we washed the dishes and strolled down to the beach. The sun was high now, and hot for the time of year, and I had discarded my jeans and roll-neck in favour of a pair of shorts made out of cut-down denims. The girls wore bikinis.

The beach was only a couple of hundred yards long, with cliffs closing it off at either end and a stream running across the middle. It was completely surrounded by my land, so there was never anyone else there. The cliffs sheltered it from the wind, so it was a real sun-trap.

We took off our clothes and ran, hand in hand, across the sand to the sea. It was icy cold, but welcome after the walk. We fooled around in the shallows, splashing one another, and the women ganged up on me and ducked my head.

We swum around for a while, enjoying the weightlessness, then walked back up the beach. The sun had almost dried us by the time we reached our clothes. Annabel lay on her back on the hot sand, arms and legs spread wide, in a typically inelegant position. I eased myself down on top of her and kissed her lips. She wriggled appreciatively.

Babs was standing beside us. I rolled off Annabel, got up on my knees, and kissed Babs' wet pubic hair.

"Come and play mothers and fathers," I said, looking up between her breasts at her face.

She took my face in her hands and shook her head. "Today I feel like watching," she said.

We lay on the beach all day, sunbathing and drinking cold lager from cans we put in a rock pool to keep cold. When we got too hot we went in the sea, and when we could summon up the energy we made love. It was a perfect day. I kept touching both of them and memorising little details: the way Annabel's breasts swung as she bent over, the shift of muscles in Babs' buttocks as she walked. We basked in the sunshine and the warmth of our love, as if it might be our last chance.

When the sun began to cool we put our clothes back on and walked across the fields to the house. We roasted the leg of lamb and opened a couple of bottles of wine. We went to bed early.

The next morning I drove into Llantisiliog for supplies. I filled up the Ferrari at the village's only garage, and stopped to pass the time of day with David Pritchard, the youngster who ran it. He loved fast cars, and I would occasionally let him drive mine, for which he worshipped me. He also worshipped Annabel.

"New car, Mr. Carstairs?" he said, wide-eyed.

"No, this is Annabel's," I answered. He whistled. His face said what more could a man want, with a bird like that who had a car like this? He lifted the bonnet and gazed adoringly at the engine while I filled the petrol tank.

"You must come for a spin one day," I said.

Quick as a flash, he said: "It's my half-day tomorrow."

"All right, I'll meet you in the Nelson at lunchtime." I screwed the petrol cap back on and he closed the bonnet.

I drove out of the filling station and parked a few yards down the street. I bought some more lager in the Nelson, and went into the grocer's for food. As I walked up to the newsagent's I noticed a dusty black Mark 10 Jaguar parked at the kerb. There were two heavily-built men in suits in it. As I passed the open window I caught a few words of earnest conversation in London accents.

They might be on holiday, I thought. But wearing suits? They could be businessmen. But they didn't look the type. And I couldn't think what business would bring two Londoners to Llantisiliog.

I went into the newsagent's and bought a *Western Mail* and 200 cigarettes. Mrs. Jones the Shop said: "Funny you coming in now, Mr. Carstairs."

"Why?" I said quickly.

"Well, I've just this minute been telling someone where to find you. A nice gentleman he was, from London. A friend of yours, although he didn't tell me his name. He wanted to pay you a surprise visit, he said." I bet he did. "He bought a map of the area," she added.

I forced a smile. "Well, thank you."

"If you're quick you might catch him now," she said.

"Right." I went out.

The Jaguar had pulled into the filling station. I

144

stepped into the phone box outside the newsagent's. I could see the garage through the windows of the kiosk. A sign over the pumps said: "Pritchard & Son, Any Make of Car Supplied. Telephone Llantisiliog 243." I found some coins and dialled the number.

I saw David leave the Jaguar and go over to his little workshop. He picked up the phone.

"This is Mr. Carstairs, David," I said. "I'm in the phone box over the road. Listen, David, this may be difficult for you to believe, but those men in the Jaguar are villains from London who are after me."

"Good God, are they?" he said excitedly. I realised he found it all too easy to believe that I was mixed up with the underworld.

"Now, I want you to do something for me. I'll have to get back to the farm, pick up Babs and Annabel, and get straight away. Can you fix their car so they can't get far?"

"Right," he said. "Let me think." There was a minute's silence. I could see the men in the Jaguar getting impatient. "I know," David said at last. "I'll cut the down hose on the radiator. On a hot day like this, they'll have a job to go five miles before she seizes up."

"Good boy," I said, and hung up.

I got into the car and drove off without waiting to see what transpired.

"We've got to move on," I told the women when I got back to the farmhouse. They were working together in the kitchen, preparing lunch. They wore aprons, something they did rarely enough for it to be a novelty, and they made a strange picture of domesticity.

"Today?" said Annabel.

"Now. You've got a minute to pack."

Babs said: "Why?"

"Two hard-looking Londoners are in the village asking where I lived," I replied grimly.

Babs said: "Oh, no." The tranquillity of the last few days left her and the old terror returned to her eyes. I took her by the shoulders.

"I'm sorry, honey," I said. "We've been kidding ourselves for the last couple of days. It's been beautiful, but unreal. I can't escape from this thing that I've started. I must finish it." She nodded dumbly.

"But I don't want you two around," I added. "I've taken you into too much danger and hurt already. Only my own head is going on the block this time."

Annabel thought for a minute, then said: "We could go to Westleigh."

"Good idea," I said. Westleigh was her father's country house in Somerset. "We'll drive down to Cardiff. I can put you on a Bristol train, then drive to town."

I walked quickly around the house closing windows and switching off electric points. As we had come unexpectedly we had next to nothing to pack, and within a minute we were getting into the car.

I drove slowly down the track. As we neared the road I saw the black Jaguar.

It went along the road past the mouth of our drive. Steam was rising from its bonnet in clouds, and it was moving in fits and starts. I speeded up.

When we got to the end of the drive the Jaguar was doing a u-turn in the road. The villains obviously had realised they had gone past the entrance. I pulled on to the main road and drove in their direction.

They must have smelled a rat, because they stopped dead in the middle of the road. I put my foot down.

As I approached the driver opened his door and put his foot on to the road—a very silly mistake. I clipped the open door with my offside wing as I shot past. I think I amputated his leg just below the knee. Then we were around the corner and away.

A couple of miles further on I stopped to inspect the damage. There was a big dent in the wing, and the headlight was smashed. But the spotlights were intact, so I was still legal. I lifted the bonnet and looked at the engine. No damage.

Annabel drove then, leaving my mind free to make plans. We crossed the Brecon Beacons in glorious sunshine. As we drove into the grimy industrial town of Merthyr Tydfil, the sky darkened to match the cheerless grey stone of the terraced houses.

It was time to play the last hand.

When I had seen Babs and Annabel off at the station I went into a call-box and dialled the Yard. I asked for Detective-Inspector Lambourne. While I waited to be put through I looked through the kiosk window at the gloomy station concourse trying—irrationally—to spot villains. Everyone looked ordinary: people buying tickets, struggling with luggage, hurrying to catch trains. The digital clock said 12:47. I adjusted my watch. A voice said: "Lambourne here."

"Arthur, it's Apples. Did you find out who's behind the Purple End?"

"Yes. Chap called Kidd. James Kidd, but they call him Cisco."

"Very humorous. Know him?"

"No convictions, but we know of him. He keeps very bad company."

"Thank you, Arthur."

"Are you going to tell me what you're up to now?"

"Sorry mate. Some time soon, eh?"

"I don't know why I bother."

"It must be my lovely nature." I hung up.

Poor Arthur. He faithfully was feeding me information, not knowing whether I was using it for good or evil ends, in the faint hope that I might come up with something. Still, if I did he would get the credit.

I filled up with petrol outside Newport and got on the M4. Traffic on the motorway was light, and I did the 140 miles to Chiswick in just over an hour. It was mad, really, but then nothing I did these days was very sane.

It was the relatively quiet after-lunch period for London traffic. I wound my way across town. I had discovered that there was no quick way to cross London, but the least slow way was to plough straight through the middle. It took me longer to get from Chiswick to Sam Green's scrap-yard than it did from Newport to London.

Sam was in the yard hut, playing poker with his son. The old sod would fleece his grandmother if she gave him a chance.

"Deal me in," I said, drawing up a chair. I

cleared several beer bottles off the stained wooden table.

"Shilling minimum," said Sam. He dealt me a hand.

For a few minutes the only words we spoke were "Raise you," "See you," and "I'm out." Sam won consistently until I moved his tobacco tin from in front of him. He had been looking at the cards he dealt reflected in the shiny underside of the tin.

"You cheating bastard," I said with a smile. His son looked amazed.

Sam shrugged. "Got to make a living," he said. I laughed.

We played on. Casually, I said: Know a geezer called Jim Kidd? Cisco, they call him."

"I have come across him, said Sam. "Matter of fact he was in here about six weeks ago. The boy fitted a nice stereo cassette player in his car. Nice car, too—a Mercedes."

"Where does he live?"

"Got a house near Aldgate. Barmouth Road. Big old place he's had done up. He's well loaded. I think he owns clubs."

"Yes, he does."

"What's your interest—he owe you money?"

"No." I thought quickly. "I'm thinking of going into that line myself. I'm wondering if he wants to sell one or two of his places."

That satisfied Sam's curiosity. We played on for a while. The business about the stereo cassette had give me an idea.

I left soon after that and drove to the Aldgate area. I stopped off to buy a cheap cassette recorder. Then I sat in the car and set it up to record. There was a demonstration tape in it.

I held the microphone to my mouth and pressed the "Record" button. "I want you to take a message to your boss, Cisco," I said. "He's got all of tomorrow to collect a million pounds in cash. If he wants to do business with me he must be at the Purple End between nine and ten tomorrow night, where I will phone him with further instructions." I rewound the tape and played it back to make sure it had recorded. Then I wound the tape back to the beginning again, took it out of the machine, and slipped it into my pocket.

I found Barmouth Road and it was easy to tell which house belonged to Kidd. It was the only one with an armed guard.

It was a detached house, not particularly grand, with a low wall outside. A white Mercedes was parked in the short drive. I parked up the road and walked back past the place. A hefty hard-nut was strolling around the outside of the house trying to pretend the bulge in his jacket was a rather large fob watch. He turned the corner of the house as I went past the drive. As soon as he was out of sight I ran quickly up to the Mercedes. I only had a couple of minutes, but it should be plenty.

The door was unlocked. I sat in the driver's seat. The cassette player was in the centre console behind the hand brake. I took out the tape which was already in there: "The Beatles—Latin Style" it was, by some obscure orchestra. Crooks always have appalling taste.

I put my own cassette into the player and switched it on, so that it would come on as soon as the ignition was fired. I put the old tape in my pocket, got out of the car, and fled.

As I dined at the Hilton Hotel I thought about that armed guard. Kidd was not a poor man, but I doubted whether he was Mr. H. or even his right-hand man. Top crooks don't have to buy cheap stolen tape decks, nor do they live in modest old houses—no matter how done up they are. I was sure Kidd normally would not rate a permanent hit man on patrol outside his house. That meant they had been expecting me—again. That damn gang must have eyes and ears everywhere.

I slept uneasily that night.

In the morning I paid my bill with my Diners' Club card, took the Ferrari to have the dents knocked out of it, and went shopping. All my clothes were at the flat, and I couldn't risk going back there, so I needed some new threads. I bought a jacket with enormous white buttons, a fancy shirt, and a pair of flared trousers with turn-ups. I told the shop assistant to throw my old clothes in the dustbin and wore the new ones out of the shop.

I picked up the car in the afternoon—the garage had done a quick job for an extra fifty quid—and drove over to the hospital. A pleasant surprise was waiting for me there.

"Your daughter regained consciousness during the night, Mr. Carstairs," the sister told me. "We think she's out of danger. It's a remarkable recovery, against all the odds. Would you like to see her?"

My heart was in my mouth as I followed the nurse down the corridor and into a single room. "You won't excite her if she's awake, will you," she cautioned.

I nodded and she went out, closing the door behind her.

Jane was lying flat on her back. Her eyes were open, and she was staring at the blank ceiling. I sat on the edge of the bed.

I hardly recognised her. She was terribly pale, and so thin the skin was drawn tight over the bones of her face. She looked twenty years older than she was.

"Jane?" I said softly.

Her head stayed still as her eyes looked at me. She managed a weak smile. "Daddy," she said.

"Honey," I said, fighting back the tears. "Why . . . How did you get into all this?"

She swallowed. "I suppose," she said weakly, then stopped for breath. "I suppose I thought it might help me find out . . . what was going on in my head." I sighed at the cliche. It explained nothing. There was no point in pressing it. She went on: "But it didn't. It's . . . it's like a car with no brakes. One you've started, there's no way to stop but crash."

"But you've done it now," I said in a broken voice. I took a deep breath. "You've crashed. Now we'll look after you until you never want that stuff any more."

She looked at me with very adult eyes then, and I

realised she knew just how little my reassurance was worth.

"Hey," I said, changing the subject. "What would you like to do when you leave hospital?" You could do anything, you know—go abroad, a cruise, Africa—you name it."

"I know just what I'd like," she said, and for the first time her eyes lit up with a spark of hope. "I'd like to live on a farm. Live simply, get up early and go to bed at half past nine. Feed chickens and milk a cow. You know."

I took her hand in mine. "Did you know I had a farm?"

She shook her head slowly.

"It's in Wales. I've just been there. A local couple raise sheep on the land, and I have an old farmhouse in a field. There's a beach nearby, too."

"Could we go there, Daddy? When I get well?" There was something childlike about her words that belied her weary middle-aged face.

"Of course we can," I said.

"I mean we, Daddy. You and I. Will you live with me for a while?"

The thought flashed briefly through my mind that Jane might get on well with David Pritchard, the Llantisiliog garage man. "You bet I will," I said. "No problems. What's the use of being rich if you can't take a couple of years off for something really important?"

She looked into my eyes with that adult gaze again. I leaned forward.

"I mean it, Jane. I really do."

The door opened behind me. I heard the sister's voice call me.

"Good-bye, Jane," I whispered. She closed her eyes.

As I walked through the disinfected hospital corridors I re-ran the conversation in my mind. All my promises to Jane had been hollow. As I had always done, I made pledges I could not guarantee to fulfil. I had small reason to think I would be alive when she got better. And if I was alive I would be lucky to be out of jail.

I got into the car and pointed it at the West End. I drove slowly, reluctant to make the next move in the game. I would have a superb dinner, I decided. The thought came unbidden into my mind: The condemned man ate a hearty breakfast. Suddenly I wanted, very badly, to back out. I was in a completely unfamiliar world, competing with experts. I was a novice draughts player taking on the world champion chessmaster. I was as good as dead.

Why had I got myself into such a mess? Jane was getting better now. I stood to lose everything I held dear, all for a foolish vengeance I had lost heart for. But I had set some very powerful machinery in motion, and I had to stay in the game until it stopped of its own accord.

It was one of those restaurants which is disguised as a solicitor's office so that the hoi polloi will not go in. The rich Victorian furnishings depressed me, and the waiters in their black jackets looked like undertakers.

I sipped my soup. It was clear and almost colourless, with a flavour so delicate you had to think about it before you could taste it. Hell, I thought, what about all the other Janes? At least I stood a chance of preventing a few hundred other kids from falling into an early grave on the point of the big needle.

I drank some wine while I waited for my steak. I had chosen champagne, and a very costly vintage, but I was already regretting it. It was a carefree, trivial drink, and what I needed was an injection of savagery.

I told the waiter to take it away and bring me a bottle of cheap burgundy.

"Cheap, sir?" he said without a trace of rebuke in his voice.

"Yes. Spanish if possible, and not too old."

"I'm afraid we do not serve Spanish wines at all, sir. However there is a house burgundy which is not too, ah, delicate."

"Fine."

He brought the wine and I tasted it. It ran rawly down my throat and started a small fire in my stomach. That was better. I cut into the two-inch fillet steak and watched the blood run out of its rare centre. My mood began to alter. It was no good my feeling like a fourth-former standing outside the headmaster's door. I had dirty work to do. I took a long swallow of the wine.

I ate no vegatables, but when I had finished the steak I ordered another one. I told the waiter: "Bring me the phone while it's cooking."

He plugged the instrument into the wall next to my table and I dialled Directory Inquiries. They gave me the number of the Purple End, and I dialled that.

It was picked up as soon as it rang.

"Carstairs," I said.

"Well?" came the voice. It sounded peculiar, as if it was muffled by a handkerchief. That meant that either Mr. H. was a very cautious bloke, or he was afraid I would recognise his voice. My nightmare came back to me, and I struggled momentarily to see the face in the dream. No good.

"Have you got the money?"

"Have you got the goods?"

"Yes," I said. "One thousand kilos of pure. Do you want it?"

"Yes."

I lowered my voice. "Have the money in a suitcase. Be at the main entrance to the Talk of the Town at half past midnight. I will pull up in a blue Ferrari and open the door. If you don't jump in quickly I'll be gone."

"How do I know I can trust you?" the muffled voice asked. I laughed.

"That's rich, from you. But you'll have your boys following you, and mine will be close by. So let's have no trickery. A mass shoot-out would ruin both of us."

"Okay." The phone went dead. Businesslike fellow, I thought.

When I had demolished the second superb steak, I skipped the melt-in-your-mouth desserts and ate a lump of Danish blue cheese. I drank whisky with it. By now the waiter must have me figured for a nutcase, I thought. But the meal, the drink and the phone call had started the old Carstairs adrenalin pumping. I felt like a fight.

The bill came to £20. The waiter probably thought anyone who paid that price for a meal was a nutcase. Maybe he was right.

As I walked along the street to the car a young lout bumped into me.

"Watch it, you stupid cunt," he said to me, mainly to impress his girl friend. It was just what I needed.

"Get lost, sonny," I snarled.

He took a wild swing at me. I swayed sideways, caught his lapel as he lurched towards me, and pushed him back against a plate-glass shop window with all my might. The window gave way and he fell right through. I walked on.

I found the car and got in. Behind the tinted windows I took off my new clothes and changed into the denims and sweater I had brought from the farm. Then I found Annabel's pistol under the dashboard, and loaded it.

I looked at my watch. It was midnight.

I put the pistol in the glove box, slipped my trusty spanner into my jacket pocket, and started the engine. As I pulled into the traffic I wondered whether it would be M. H. himself who would meet me. A top villain would hardly dirty his hands by pulling off a dope deal in person, but on the other hand a million greenies was a lot of cash to entrust to an underling.

At 12:25 I circled Trafalgar Square and drove north up Charing Cross Road. I stopped at a zebra crossing and a red traffic light. It was 12:31 when I stopped on a double yellow line outside the Talk of the Town and opened the passenger door.

A man in a hat carrying a small executive briefcase stepped quickly from the club entrance. He put his head inside the car and looked into the back seat before getting in.

In a moment he had slammed the door and we were moving away. He steadied the briefcase on his knees.

His hair under the hat was silver, and he had a small white moustach . His dark suit was expensively cut in an old-fashioned style, and he wore a striped club tie.

I drove east. "Open the case," I told him. He did so. It was packed with large-denomination notes.

"All right," I said.

"And what about your part of the deal?" he asked.

I had wanted him to speak. His accent was Home Countries, and sounded genuine. If I hadn't known better I would have put him down as a middle-ranking civil servant.

"You're going to see it soon," I told him. "There'll be no trouble."

"I should hope not," he replied. "You've caused enough trouble already."

I concealed the slight pleasure that statement gave me. "You shouldn't have chased me about so much," I said. "I only wanted to do a little business with you."

"But you were trouble anyway. You can't buy that much stuff without upsetting the market, you know." He might have been talking to his stockbroker about the commodity market.

"How did I upset the market?" I had to draw him out. If I kept him talking he might give me the clue I needed to decide whether he was Mr. H. or not.

"You caused the biggest shortage in two years," he replied. "You cleaned out our suppliers and the price rocketed. The punters were getting desperate, the pushers were getting shirty, and we began to lose our grip on the business. We all got orders to mix the junk to make it go further, and the junkies found out . . . we were being squeezed from both ends."

Now I knew. "We got orders . . . we were squeezed from both ends." It meant this chap was an underling. A fairly highranker, no doubt, but not my man. I cursed silently. My gamble had failed, and I had run out of ideas. I was stumped.

Still I had to go on with the charade. I pulled into the lane behind Crown Terrace and stopped the car outside the back of No. 17. "Well, here is the answer to your problems," I told the man.

We got out and went into the garage. I switched on the lights and pointed to the drums. "One million pounds worth of death," I said.

He rubbed his hands, and in his eyes I saw the light of greed which made the difference between him and a middle-ranking civil servant.

"Would you like to count the money while I test the stuff?" he asked.

"Yes."

"Good," he said. "I'll get my case from the car. He went back out.

I started to open one of the drums. I unwound the tape, took off the lid, and lifted out a polythene sack. I wondered what arrangement the gang would make for picking the stuff up. Maybe the civil servant would ring up and give the address, and they would send a lorry down. More likely, they had a van following us and it was just waiting for the go-ahead now.

I didn't see how I could get a lead on Mr. H.

before the deal was completed. Following the fellow who brought the money would be far too predictable. I could hang around and tag on to whoever collected the dope, but that was not much better.

Or I could tell Lambourne all I knew and leave it to him. I knew how the stuff was coming in, where it changed hands, and the central distribution point. Lambourne could set a trap. Perhaps he wouldn't get Mr. H., but at least the racket would be smashed.

I was wondering where the civil servant type had got to when I heard footsteps behind me. Without turning I said: "When will you take the stuff away—now or later?"

"Right now," said a strange voice. I spun around. Two complete strangers stood just inside the garage door. One of them said: "Detective-Sergeant Dennis, Scotland Yard. You are under arrest."

CHAPTER SIXTEEN

I sat in my cell and tried to figure it out. It didn't make sense any way I looked at it. Why had the gang double-crossed me this way? They had kept their money, presumably, but they still didn't have the heroin. If they had to get rid of me, why didn't they dream up some way of bumping me off and keeping the dope?

And how had the thing been set up? Was my civil-servant type a policeman? An informer? How could the police co-operate with a gang like that?

It was a complete puzzle. Once again, I had jumped in at the deep end only to find I was not as strong a swimmer as I had thought. I had failed in every purpose. Mr. H. was free and completely unknown to me. I had invested over £100,000 in a lousy deal. And now the police would never credit my account of the heroin racket.

But the immediate problem was that I was in jail, and looked like staying there. The evidence against me must be pretty strong, I thought. My fingerprints would be all over the drums, and I had been caught red-handed opening one. The more I thought about it, the worse it got. Sooner or later I would be connected with the car in which Guy died—the white Citroen. Then there was my getting booked for speeding on my first trip to Marseilles. Oh, and the stamps on my passport.

A half-way intelligent detective would have the whole thing pieced together in no time at all. And with the quantity of stuff they had found, I would go down for a long, long stretch.

I paced up and down the cell and tried to figure out a story to tell my solicitor, who I had called half an hour ago. I would have to say either that I did not know the stuff was heroin, or that I did not know it was there. Or both. Shit, I needed a long time to figure it all out. I would have to stall him for tonight.

There were footsteps in the corridor and the jailer opened the cell door. "Your solicitor is here," he said. "On your feet."

I didn't think he had any right to be rude to me

until after I was convicted. "Do you miss the Army, corporal?" I said pleasantly. An angry light flashed behind his eyes, and I knew I had scored a bullseye with that shot.

I sat in the interview room and my solicitor was brought in. He was about fifty, with a near-bald head, and although it was three a.m. he was immaculately dressed in a grey suit and silver tie. He carried a briefcase, but what he could have in it that might be relevant to my plight I could not imagine.

He looked around him at the dirty grey walls and the bare table and chairs which were the room's only furniture, and made a grimace of distaste. "It's a long time since I've been in one of these places," he said conversationally.

"Me, too," I said abruptly. "Sit down." He was more used to dealing with company law than with criminal cases, and I wondered if he would be any good. I would probably have to tell him what to say.

"The first thing we have to worry about," I said, "is getting me out of here."

I was led into the magistrates court at 11:30 the next morning. My solictior was up front, and in the public gallery was Richard Elliott, who was going to go bail for me.

If I could get bail, that was. I had spent several house of the night talking about just that with my solicitor. He had told me: "The only reason for refusing bail is that there is a likelihood the accused will abscond."

"That's the theory," I told him. But I had spent more time in magistrates' courts than he had. "In

162

practice they'll jail you if they think you're guilty, or violent, or a layabout, or if the police press hard enough." Then I had told him exactly what to say.

I looked about the court. There was one fellow in the Press bench. Fortunately I didn't know him. No doubt he worked for a local paper and did lineage for the nationals. With a bit of luck he would not recognise my name.

I looked at the Justices. The Chairman of the Bench was a fat old dodderer with three chins and a crumpled suit. A middle-aged lady in a ridiculous hat sat on one side of him, and on the other was a chinless wonder who was probably a local politician.

A police sergeant in uniform stood up. "Charge number eighteen on your lists, your worships," he said. "Chadwell James Carstairs, possession of dangerous drugs, namely one kilogram of heroin. There is an additional charge, not on your list, of possessing a firearm without a licence. I am instructed to ask for a remand in custody for seven days. The police are opposing bail because of the serious nature of the charge, and because there are other matters to be investigated."

I was puzzled. Why was there only one kilo of heroin on the charge? My solicitor stood up.

"I am asking for bail for my client, your worships," he said. I had to admit he looked and sounded impressive. And the fact that he was a stranger to the Court—and looked as if he would be more at home in the High Court—would go in my favour. Most of the villains were defended by a handful of local lawyers who had got a corner in the criminal work. The fact that I had my own lawyer marked me as a cut above the run of defendants from the start.

"He is a highly respectable man," my solicitor went on. "He has never been in trouble with the police, apart from a minor case in the juvenile court in 1942. He is a man with heavy responsibilities and a director of several companies which would suffer from a prolonged absence on his part." At this the reporter pricked up his ears, but he was hard-nosed enough to know that a company director could mean a self-employed decorator.

"The police have told you they are still investigating this matter, and unless they drop the charges the case is certain to go to the Central Criminal Court. A remand in custody would mean my client spending several months in jail.

"The charges are indeed serious, your worships, but my client has a complete answer to them and intends to plead not guilty. I know it is not my business here and now to go into the details of the case, but I think I ought to tell your worships this.

"The drugs in question were found on property which is owned by one of the companies of which my client is a director. The firearm in the second charge does not belong to him, but was found in a borrowed car he was driving.

"In the light of this, I would respectfully submit that it would be quite wrong to remand my client in custody. I ask your worships to grant bail. A surety is present—my client's accountant—and is in court at the moment.

"I do not think I can help your worships any further."

The magistrates went into a huddle. I was still

puzzling over why only one kilo of heroin was mentioned in the charge. Of course, the police could amend the charge later with no trouble at all. But they would have had a better chance of keeping me in custody if they had put the full amount in.

Suddenly I had a wild idea. My head began to spin with the crazy implications of it. But the chairman of the bench was speaking.

"There will be a remand for seven days," he said. As he leaned forward I noticed that the disgusting old twit was dribbling slightly from the corner of his mouth. "Bail will be granted in the sum of £500 and with a surety of £500."

I was free. And I had a lot to do.

I left the court in a cold rage—rage that I had been betrayed, and rage that I had been too blind to see it. I knew I was capable of murder in that mood, and I did not care.

I drove to Sloane Square and parked in a meter bay thirty yards from the entrance to the block of flats. All the pieces of the jigsaw had now fallen into place. I should have known who Mr. H. was right from the start—from my first visit to the Purple End. If I had missed that, the Coitroen should have clinched it. Or the armed guard at Kidd's house. I had been walking around with blinkers on.

I killed the engine and sat in the car. It was another hot day, and the heat rose in shimmering air-currents from the tarmac. Englishmen in their ridiculous suits hurried along the pavement, ties and collars undone to ventilate their sweating bodies. I lit a cigarette, looked at my watch, and settled down to wait. If I was right—and I had to be—Mr. H. would come down the steps from the flats some time. It might not be today, but I could wait. I had seven days, but I did not think I would need them all.

I knew now how the gang had worked that caper last night. They had their heroin at last, and I thought that what the civil servant type had told me was probably true—there was a chronic shortage. That, and greed, would mean they would be in a hurry to get their new supplies on to the market.

The Sloane Square flat was the lynch-pin of the whole racket. It provided a buffer between the English and French ends of the operation. And Mr. H. had to operate the connection himself. He had to be the one who picked up the stuff and left the money. He had to be Miss Dunhill's other caller. That way no one else could aspire to take over the operation. And there was a very special reason why the police would never get on to the flat.

I lit another cigarette and threw the empty packet out of the window. I left the window down, to let out some of the car's stuffy air. The sun moved around the sky until the car was blessed with the shadow of the building.

When he finally came out I almost missed him. I was searching the dashboard shelf for a fresh packet of cigarettes when a sixth sense made me lift my head and look through the windscreen.

Down the steps, in his trendy suit and kipper tie, carrying a briefcase, came Detective-Inspector Arthur Lambourne—the bastard.

I fumbled with the door handle, got it open, and stumbled out of the car on to the pavement.

"Lambourne!" I yelled.

He turned and looked at me, an expression of

blank astonishment on his face. Then he started to run. I made after him until he stopped and jumped into an orange Lotus Europa parked at the kerb. I saw he was too far ahead for me to catch him. I turned and sprinted back to the Ferrari.

I jumped in and started the engine. It roared as I stamped on the accelerator.

The Lotus was pointing the opposite way from my car. It pulled out from the kerb and shot past me. A mini coming towards us braked hard to miss him, slewed around and skidded, and crashed into a parked car.

My tyres screamed as I pulled away in a tight u-turn and shot after Lambourne. He had a start of about 100 yards by now, but if I could keep him in sight I could catch him.

He crossed a set of traffic lights. As I approached them they switched to amber. I flicked the headlights on and leaned on the horn. The lights changed to red. I saw the nose of a car ease forward on my left-hand side as I shot across the junction. I changed into second gear and sounded the horn again. A beat bobby watched wide-eyed as I passed, then lifted his pocket walkie-talkie. Good—the more attention I got, the less chance Lambourne had of getting away and denying the whole thing ever happened.

Still I had to keep on his tail. I was doing the wild, insane speed of 110 miles per hour down a London street now, and I pushed from my mind the thought of what might happen if a pedestrian stepped in front of me.

Suddenly Lambourne's brake-lights flashed; I stamped on the brakes and went into a straight-line skid. He slewed around into a right turn and went down a side street. My speed dropped fast, but I was still doing 60 m.p.h. when I reached the corner. I fought with the stubborn wheel for a fraction of a second: I felt the back of the car start to slip; then grip again. I mounted the far pavement of the side street and missed a lamp-post by a whisker. Then I was back in second gear and tearing off after the Lotus again.

I smelled burning. I glanced in my rear-view mirror and saw smoke clouding the street. I wondered where it could be coming from, then I realised. It was my tyres. Fuck them.

A quarter of a mile further down the side street led into a main road. A lady warden was directing traffic. She held up her hand to stop the Lotus and wave on the cars in the main road.

Lambourne ignored her, scraped past her by an inch and heaved right again. One of the cars she had called on braked, swerved, and grazed the wing of the Lotus. The orange car wobbled perilously then righted. All the traffic stopped, leaving me a clear junction. I screeched around the bend.

I was right on the swine's tail now. I could see his face reflected in his rear-view mirror, a mask of desperation: the face of a man who thought he had won the game then discovered there was another round to fight. Somewhere a police siren began to wail. I almost had him.

There was a roundabout ahead, blocked up with traffic at a standstill. The tail lights flashed again. The entrance to the roundabout was blocked. The Lotus swerved to the right and mounted the central reservation. Incredibly, Lambourne regained control as the car landed on the wrong side of the road.

A car came out of the roundabout at the Lotus and swerved around it. With my heart in my mouth, I copied Lambourne's desperate manoeuvre. There was a stomach-blow from the Ferrari's suspension as the front hit the high kerb of the central reservation. Then I was over.

Lambourne saw his gap in the traffic and shot into the roundabout. But the next exit was choked with traffic. Instead of turning into the roundabout he went straight at the central green island. The Lotus leapt into the air, landed in a flowerbed, spat mud and catapulted forward again. I gritted my teeth and followed.

He went straight ahead, out of the far side of the junction. Then he saw the trap.

Three police cars, their blue lights turning impassively, blocked the width of the road.

He turned suddenly into a narrow side road on the left. But he had made a bad mistake. On either side of the little street were market stalls, leaving hardly enough room for a slow car to pass through the middle.

He braked hard, but hopelessly, and crashed into a fruit stall. Women screamed, and peaches and bananas flew everywhere. The stall was pushed along the road into the next one. The Lotus spun around so that the driver's door faced me as I skidded around the corner. Lambourne leapt out, briefcase in hand.

I kept right on going.

I must have hit him at about 40 m.p.h. His legs were crushed mercilessly between the bonnet of my car and the side of the Lotus. His face screwed up in

169

an expression of terror and pain, he threw up his hands and fell forward on to my bonnet. The briefcase sailed through the air and landed on the pavement. As it hit the ground it burst, scattering a fine white powder over the flagstones.

CHAPTER SEVENTEEN

I had a nasty crack on my forehead where it had hit on the inside of the car just above the windscreen. I had no right to be conscious, but I fought the waves of nausea and the insistent darkness which tried to close around my eyes, and struggled out of the car.

The police already had arrived. I staggered up to an inspector and held on to his broad shoulder for support.

"You're in a bad way . . . " I interrupted him.

"Listen. See that . . . " I pointed at the white powder spilling out of the briefcase. "That is pure heroin. There's more of it—a million pounds worth—at No. 11, Sloane Mansion, just off Sloane Square." He turned away. "Wait," I said. I had visions of a quick call to the Yard, and a bunch of bent coppers from Lambourne's own squad racing around to destroy the evidence. "There's not much time," I said. "Be quick." That might ensure that the raid was carried out by the local nick, my failing brain thought as it slipped into darkness. I was out before I hit the ground.

There was something cool on my forehead when I came around. I unglued my eyes and saw Babs. I tried to turn my head—and a sharp pain across my temples quickly changed my mind.

"You gave your head a nasty carck," said Annabel's voice.

"You should see the other guy," I joked weakly.

"He's dead," she said.

"Good," I said, and went back to sleep.

When I woke up again I realised I was in hospital. I lay on white sheets, surrounded by hideous floral-patterend curtains. I put my hand to my head, and my fingers met a thick bandage.

Either side of the white bed sat Annabel and Babs, looking very worried. I said: "You can take off your funeral faces and break out the champagne. We won."

Annabel said: "You took long enough to come round."

I frowned. The sun was still streaming in through a window behind my left shoulder. "It's not dark yet," I said.

"The accident was yesterday," she replied.

"Oh." It took a moment for that to sink in. Then I said: "Anyway, it was no accident."

Babs said: "But Apples . . . Lambourne?"

I nodded, and immediately regretted it as the pain shot across my forehead again. "Yes," I said when it had subsided. "Lambourne was Mr. H. I should have seen it ages ago. Remember the first time we went to the Purple End?"

"I won't forget that in a hurry."

"They were expecting us. The trap was set and I walked into it. But who could have warned them I

171

was going there? Only two people could have known. The punk who was living with Jane knew I was after Harry Hat, because he gave me the name. But he said nothing about the club. And he could not warn the gang about me without letting on that he had put me on to them—and he would be too frightened to do that.

"The only other person who knew I was going there was Lambourne. I asked him where I could find Harry Hat, and he told me the Purple End. He must have warned them to expect me.

"But the clincher was the Citroen." I stopped for a moment and my dream came back to me in a flood. I knew now why I had shouted out about the Citroen. "When the gang was after the heroin I brought from France, they ambushed the hired Citroen that Guy was driving. Now how could they have known the stuff might be coming over in that car?

"I hired the car in Paris. When I picked up the dope in Marseilles it was loaded into a Fiat. Only Guy knew about the Citroen—and one other person."

"Who?" asked Babs.

"A hitch-hiker I picked up when I came off the ferry. She stepped on to the roadside and started thumbing as I hit the main road. She was with me when I changed cars in Paris.

"She must have been working for the gang. But how did they know I was going to France on that day, by that particular ferry? Once again, only one person knew.

"Before I left I phoned Lambourne. He asked me to ring him later in the day, and I said, "I can't.

I'm catching the six o'clock ferry from Dover." He must have sent the girl to Calais with instructions to thumb a lift with me and stay with me as long as possible. She must have told him about the Citroen.

"I didn't see it until the court this morning."

Annabel interrupted: "Yesterday morning."

"Oh yes. Anyway, in court I was only charged with possessing one kilo of heroin. I had been trying to figure out how the gang could hope to profit from double-crossing me and grassing. The idea occurred to me that one or two of the police might be bent, and they had passed the dope on to the gang. Once that idea struck me, everything else suddenly fell into place.

"I already thought the Sloane Square flat was the centre of the operation. Normally, Robins took the stuff there and Lambourne picked it up. It had to be Lambourne. He had the same kind of immunity as Robins; and he wouldn't want another soul to know about the place—it would have been too risky.

"Because that was their safe house, it was the only place they could take the heroin they got from me. And they had to get some of it on to the market quickly. So Lambourne went there for a consignment in the afternoon, and I caught him redhanded. The end."

There was silence for a while. Talking had tired me. Babs was nervously twisting her rings.

Annabel said: "Apples—" and stopped.

"Not now, honey," said Babs.

But I had seen this coming. "It's all right," I said softly. "It's been in your eyes all the time. I've just been talking to postpone the inevitable. You want out, don't you."

173

I did not blame them. The last few weeks had brought about an irreversible change in our relationship.

"The things that used to hold us together have driven us apart," I said. "You've seen the real me, for the first time—bitter, vengeful and ruthless. I'm not any good as security for you now. I've brought you pain and fear; and you know it could happen again."

"Oh, no, you've got it all back to front," said Babs.

I laughed. "As usual."

"You see—I've changed too. All my life I've been terrified of the men who come in the night to take me by force. Now it's happened—and the fear is gone. I'm ready to stand on my own." She smiled a sad smile. "Look at the fort I've built around me to protect me from the world. Not just a man to love me—but a man and a woman, rich people. White people.

"The world is hard, especially for an ordinary Jamaican girl. But I don't want to escape it any more. I want to fight it.

"It doesn't sound very impressive, does it. But it makes sense to me."

I said: "It makes sense to me, too." I looked at Annabel. "You too?"

"It wouldn't work, you and me, Apples," she said. She was right.

"You stuck with me when I needed you," I said. "Now you are free. I don't mind. It's been good, loving you both."

"What will happen to you now?" Babs asked.

"Well, Lambourne's pals will be investigated and

174

prosecuted. I'll have to give evidence. They may prosecute me, too—I've broken enough laws. If they do I reckon I'll get a suspended sentence. But most likely they won't bother, especially as I'll be so much help to them."

"And afterwards?" Annabel whispered.

"I'm going to live with Jane for a while, on the farm. It's what she wants, and it will do her a lot of good. I could do with a year or two of doing nothing, too. I shall paint."

They nodded. There was an embarrassing silence.

"There's no more to say," I told them. "Kiss me now, and push off."

They did.

A little while later a nurse came in and drew the curtains across the window.

ACTION ADVENTURE

SILENT WARRIORS (1675, $3.95)
by Richard P. Henrick
The Red Star, Russia's newest, most technologically advanced submarine, outclasses anything in the U.S. fleet. But when the captain opens his sealed orders 24 hours early, he's staggered to read that he's to spearhead a massive nuclear first strike against the Americans!

THE PHOENIX ODYSSEY (1789, $3.95)
by Richard P. Henrick
All communications to the USS *Phoenix* suddenly and mysteriously vanish. Even the urgent message from the president cancelling the War Alert is not received. In six short hours the *Phoenix* will unleash its nuclear arsenal against the Russian mainland.

COUNTERFORCE (2013, $3.95)
Richard P. Henrick
In the silent deep, the chase is on to save a world from destruction. A single Russian Sub moves on a silent and sinister course for American shores. The men aboard the U.S.S. *Triton* must search for and destroy the Soviet killer Sub as an unsuspecting world races for the apocalypse.

EAGLE DOWN (1644, $3.75)
by William Mason
To western eyes, the Russian Bear appears to be in hibernation— but half a world away, a plot is unfolding that will unleash its awesome, deadly power. When the Russian Bear rises up, God help the Eagle.

DAGGER (1399, $3.50)
by William Mason
The President needs his help, but the CIA wants him dead. And for Dagger—war hero, survival expert, ladies man and mercenary extraordinaire—it will be a game played for keeps.

Available wherever paperbacks are sold, or order direct from the Publisher. Send cover price plus 50¢ per copy for mailing and handling to Zebra Books, Dept. 2776, 475 Park Avenue South, New York, N.Y. 10016. Residents of New York, New Jersey and Pennsylvania must include sales tax. DO NOT SEND CASH.